Chameleon
Dad

Chameleon Dad

Debbie Thomas

Little
Island
Books create waves

CHAMELEON DAD
First published in 2022 by
Little Island Books
7 Kenilworth Park
Dublin 6W
Ireland

First published in the USA by Little Island Books in 2023

Print ISBN: 978-1-91241-788-9

Cover illustration by Shannon Bergin
Designed and typeset by Rosa Devine
Edited by Siobhán Parkinson
Copyedited by Emma Dunne
Printed in Poland by Drukarnia Skleniarz

Little Island has received funding to support this book
from the Arts Council of Ireland.

10 9 8 7 6 5 4 3 2 1

For my brave and beautiful sister Jo

1. A Lovely Shade of Bread

Connie was choosing her dad. She'd narrowed him down to two. The first possibility had just walked through the sliding doors. He crossed the Arrivals area and stopped under the 'Welcome to Dublin Airport' sign. He frowned as he looked around, as if he'd been expecting someone to meet him off the plane. He had straight hair the colour of Nutella, just like Connie's. He wore a dark blue suit and pointy brown shoes.

The second possible dad stood waiting behind the barrier rail. He'd been there for fifteen minutes. That had given Connie plenty of time to size him up from her chair behind a pillar in the Pie in the Sky café. His hair was a quarrel of greying curls but his eyes were like hers, round and shiny-brown, as if a conker had been stuck in each socket.

Connie imagined life with each of them.

First Dad would leave every morning at seven and get home after six, but he'd make up for it with holidays in Tenerife. They'd stay in big hotels with tiny bottles of moon-coloured bubble bath you could take home.

With Second Dad she'd live half-way up a mountain in a cottage as scruffy as he was. They'd breed llamas and make their own ice cream, go skiing in winter and climbing in summer.

Connie liked bubble bath. But she preferred ice cream, and definitely mountains. She'd just settled on Second Dad when the Arrivals doors slid open again. A woman came through, hand in hand with a little girl. The man ducked under the barrier rail, ran over and scooped the child into his arms.

How wonderful! thought Connie, with an ache of gladness for the girl. Pressing her lips together, she turned to First Dad. He must have given up on being met because he was walking towards the exit. He looked her way and stopped.

Her heart gave a hop. No. After all these years, could he actually be ...?

But the look on his face didn't say, 'Crikey Mikey, it's my long-lost daughter.' It said, 'Holy Himalayas, what's that?'

Connie looked down. *Oh no.* Her jumping heart must have woken Hue. The chameleon had been dozing against her chest. But now his head poked out from the neck of her hoodie. 'Down!' she whispered, trying to push him back into his pouch. Too late. He kind of slid, kind of dived from under her hoodie and landed with clattery claws on the floor. He rattled across the tiles and climbed up the leg of the next-door table, where an elderly lady sat eating a muffin. She gasped as Hue stopped by her plate to catch his breath, his little stomach pumping in and out.

Connie sprang from her chair and lunged for Hue. He wriggled away over the lady's arm. She shrieked, spluttering crumbs, and shook him off. He scuttled down the table leg and across the floor, jerking this way and that like a badly made cartoon.

Connie was the only person in sixth class who could do the splits both ways. And she'd been the first to the top of the climbing wall on the school tour to Barrymore Park. But her agility couldn't match Hue's. He scurried to the pillar in front of her table. Grasping a wire that ran up the side, he climbed. At the top of the pillar he stopped and turned his head, as if daring Connie to follow him.

Don't move, she begged him silently. She dragged a chair over, stood on it and wrapped her arms round the pillar. She clasped her legs round too, then pulled herself up, as if climbing a palm tree for coconuts. Her arms hugged, her feet pushed and her knees bent out like a frog's.

At the top of the pillar, she stretched out a hand towards Hue. 'Gotcha!' she muttered. But he dodged her grasp and climbed across from the pillar on to a metal beam that ran below the ceiling. He perched on top, just beyond her reach.

Connie grabbed the beam with one hand, then the other, and swung across. Hanging like a monkey, she broke her first rule of climbing: *Don't look down*. Down was a long way away. Down was a tiled white floor with specks that winked like wicked eyes, urging her to let go. Down was a gaggle of coffee-drinking, croissant-eating customers staring up from their tables in silent wonder.

Connie's hands went clammy. They slipped round the beam. The ground-eyes begged her to fall. *Don't look down*, she told herself. *Look up.*

Above her, Hue had reached the end of the beam. He turned his head and eyed her snootily from the far wall, as if to say, 'What *you* need is a tail, my dear.' Then he stretched out his own long tail and coiled it round a pipe that ran down the wall. His legs and body followed. He scooted down the pipe and on to the counter of the Pie in the Sky café.

Connie couldn't follow that. She swung her feet back to clasp the pillar again. Then she walked her hands along the beam, hugged the pillar and slid down to the floor.

More people had joined First Dad and the café crowd to stare at Hue. He was now creeping along the counter towards a plate of scones. Thank goodness the café man had turned his back to make coffee at the noisy, hissing machine.

Across the hall, Second Dad turned to stare too.

His little daughter broke free from his grasp and ran over. 'Dragon baby!' she squealed, pointing at Hue.

'Chameleon,' Connie corrected her, pushing through the people to the counter. As if to prove it, Hue climbed on top of the scones and turned a lovely shade of bread. Someone in the crowd gasped. Someone else clapped.

The café man spun round. 'Oy! Off me cakes, you little monster.' He grabbed a phone from his pocket, jabbed it and held it to his ear. 'Mags?' he snapped. 'That girl of yours ... you'd better get down here!'

The audience had grown into a giggling, gossiping mass. 'Who needs the zoo?' someone said.

'Ten likes already.'

'This'll go viral.'

'That thing'll *give* us a virus.'

Still perching on the scones, Hue darkened to toast. Connie reached across the counter. He crept on to her hand and up her arm. She could feel him trembling through her sleeve.

'Please,' she mumbled, 'give him some space. He's shy – doesn't like crowds.' She swallowed. He wasn't the only one. She took in the group of delighted, disgusted and everything-in-between faces. *Stop staring* ... her face was on fire ... *and glaring* ... her hands felt sticky ... *and laughing and—*

''Scuse me.' A voice broke through the crowd. 'Let me through, please. I'm airport staff. Everything's under control. Stand back there. Thank you.'

Relief swept through Connie as Mags appeared in front of her. Safe, sensible, sort-it-out Mags. She grabbed Connie's hand and led her through the crowd, clearing their path like a snowplough. They crossed the hall to the lifts.

'For Pete's sake!' Mags said, as she jabbed the lift button. 'What on earth is Hue doing here? Dave called me down – said he'd agreed to keep an eye on *you* this morning, not a flippin' lizard.'

Away from the crowd, Connie's breathing calmed. Hue relaxed too in her arms. His dull-brown body went green. His legs turned red.

'I thought it would be OK,' she said, 'as long as Hue stayed in his pouch. I made it from my pillowcase.' She reached inside her hoodie and pulled out a bag on a string round her neck. 'I hid him because I thought you wouldn't let him come.'

'Too right, missy!' With her big round face and cross little eyes, Mags looked like an angry teacake. 'Put him back in there right now. He's caused enough rumpus without more people seeing.'

The lift arrived with a ping. Mags strode inside. 'Why in heaven's name did you bring him to the airport?'

As the lift rose, Connie eased Hue into the pouch. She put it gently back under her hoodie, careful not to tangle it with the chain of her locket, her most precious possession (apart from Hue, of course, if you could call him a possession, which you most certainly couldn't). 'I wanted him with me. Coming back here for the first time. In case I felt a bit ... you know.'

'Ah.' Mags blinked. 'Sure.' Her face softened. 'Right so.'

Of course she knew. Because she was the one who'd found Connie eight years ago sitting in the café: a too-small girl on a too-big chair, swinging her legs while her dad went to get her a drink.

And never came back.

2. A String Vest of a Memory

The lift doors opened on the fifth floor.

'You can wait in the cleaners' break room,' Mags said gently. She could never stay angry with Connie for long. 'It's quiet in there.' She led the way down the corridor. 'But keep Hue in his pouch in case anyone comes in.' She opened a door on the left. 'Will you be all right, love?'

'Grand.' Connie looked round the room, a muddle of chairs, tables, coffee cups and newspapers.

'There's biscuits in the cupboard.' Mags pointed to a kitchen area on the left. 'And TV over there.' She waved towards a screen on the right-hand wall. 'I must get back to work. Text if you need me. I'm cleaning in Departures on the first floor.' She went to go, then turned back again. 'Oh, love.' She drew Connie into a hug full of worry and lemon cleaning spray. 'I know this is hard. Your first time in the airport since—'

'Aah, careful of Hue!' Connie pulled away. 'I'm fine, really. Especially with him here. Though I wish you'd let me stay at home.'

'I told you,' said Mags. 'Janey's on holiday.'

Connie rolled her eyes. 'And I told *you* I don't need a minder. I'm twelve years old. Ciara stays home when her mum's at work, and she's two months younger than me.' Actually, Connie's best friend was only allowed to stay home if her older brother was around, and she was one month and fourteen days younger, but it wouldn't help to mention that right now.

'What Ciara does is her mum's business,' Mags said firmly. 'What you do is mine.'

Except you're not my mum, Connie managed not to reply.

But the thought must have leaked on to her face because Mags's shoulders sagged. 'See you at one, love,' she said. 'And promise you'll keep Hue in his pouch.'

'Mm.' Which was a noise, not a promise. So when Mags had gone, and Connie took him out, it wasn't a lie either. He would love exploring in here.

'Careful,' she said as his little foot caught in her locket chain. She untangled it and set him on the floor. 'There you go.'

He stood as still as a brooch while his eyes did the rounds of the room, darting in different directions at the same time. One eye went up while the other went down. Then one looked ahead while the other looked behind. Slowly the chameleon lifted a front leg and began his wonky old-man walk across the carpet. He was heading for a pot plant that stood on the floor against the far wall. Beside it was a stack of open lockers. Each locker had a name at the bottom – Peter, Sue, Tom, Maura – and there was Mags.

Hue reached the pot. He began to climb the plant's thick stem towards a burst of spiky leaves at the top. Half-way up he paused to survey the room, like a mountaineer enjoying the view.

Connie sat at a table. She unzipped the big pocket at the front of her hoodie and took out a pen and notebook. Opening the notebook on the table, she wrote:

July 2nd

Dear Dad,

I hope you're well. I'm fine, in case you're wondering. I'm writing this from Dublin Airport. Remember that?

Hue escaped in the café just now. You can imagine the fuss. Oh, and I saw you twice this morning. Ha, just kidding. Because the real you would have run up and hugged me for eight years. That's what you owe me, Dad. And you'd better do it soon, otherwise I might decide

She stopped writing. She'd never decide she didn't want to see him. And she was beginning to sound cross, which might put him off. She chewed the end of her pen. Put him off what? He'd never reply. Just like he'd never replied to the other hundreds of letters she'd written ever since she could spell 'Dad'.

She put the pen down. OK, she hadn't actually *sent* any of them. But how could she? She didn't know his address. And anyway, wasn't it *his* job to contact *her* after what had happened?

She put her elbows on the table. What *had* happened? That was the problem; she couldn't remember. At least, not completely. Or even mostly. The memory was like a string vest: thin threads between big holes in her mind.

She picked up the pen.

What I remember:
1. The ladybird coat I was wearing with the hood up, even though we were inside, because I loved the way the antennae poked out.
2. Sitting on a chair with my feet not reaching the ground.
3. Hue's travel box on the table.
4. A mug of hot chocolate in front of me with worms floating on top.

That's what the mini-marshmallows had looked like to her four-year-old eyes. And when her four-year-old teeth had sunk into their pale sweetness, they'd squashed like worms too. That's why she'd spat them out on the table.

5. You sitting opposite me and saying don't worry, you'd get me another drink.

6. You going to the counter and talking to the cleaning lady who was sweeping the floor. Then walking away. For ever.

Mags had told the story from her side: how a man had come up while she was sweeping. How he'd asked if she'd look after his daughter while he went to the bathroom. How she'd given out to him for wanting to leave his child with a stranger. How he'd said please, he was in a bad way because his wife had recently passed away and he didn't want his Connie to see him cry. How Mags and her big soft heart had said there now, sure she'd mind little Connie. And how she'd been minding her – and Hue, who she'd found in the travel box – ever since.

Connie could hardly remember Dad's face. Except for the glasses. He'd definitely worn glasses.

Maybe.

'Do you remember him, Huey?' She looked across the room. The chameleon had reached the top of the plant. He clung to the spiky leaves like a rainbow hairclip.

His head jerked towards her then away.

Was that a no?

Don't be ridiculous, she told herself. *His brain's the size of a Tic Tac. As if he could understand a word.*

She closed the notebook and looked at her watch. Three-quarters of an hour till Mags finished.

This was the moment when any normal twelve-year-old would take out her phone and go on Instagram or TikTok or any other app you weren't allowed to use until you were thirteen. But Connie wasn't a normal twelve-year-old. Or rather Mags wouldn't let her be.

'Not yet,' she'd say, whenever Connie asked her for a smartphone. And 'Nonsense,' she'd reply when Connie protested that everyone else in the school – and actually the world – had one. 'Even if they did, it wouldn't mean that *you* could. The Internet's bad for your health, your safety, your sleep ...' Connie half expected her to add, 'and your teeth'. So she had to make do with a stupid-phone, a great goofy slab you could only use for phoning or texting, so that Mags could always contact her at school or Ciara's house or even – which had happened once – on the loo.

There were footsteps outside the door. *Oh, no.* Connie ran over to Hue, still perched on the plant. She lifted him off. The door handle turned. There was no time to put him back inside her hoodie. She turned to the stack of lockers. 'It's OK,' she whispered, feeling him tremble on her palm. She found the locker labelled 'Mags' and slid him inside, past a box of tissues, a hairbrush, a pot of hand cream and other bits of clutter. She pulled her hands out, turned round and leaned back against the opening.

Just in time.

The door opened and a woman came in. Or rather a scowl with a woman wrapped round it.

3. Dear Connie

'You must be Mags's girl.' The woman had plum-coloured hair and a squashed-up mouth like a prune. 'Causing trouble, I hear.' She walked over to the kitchen area and opened the cupboard. She removed a packet of Bourbon biscuits and slid one into her mouth, gripping the rest in a non-offery way. Not that Connie could have gone over to take one. She had to keep her back against the locker.

Prune-mouth worked her way through the biscuit. 'Lizard on the loose, eh? Revolting creatures. Where is it now?' Her eyes flickered round the room.

'They, um ...' Connie leaned back harder, 'they took it away.' Lame, but it was all she could think of. And it did the trick.

'Ah.' The prune mouth flattened into a smile. 'Joe'll know what to do. Put the thing down if he's got any sense.'

Thing? Down? Connie leaned back even harder. She wished Joe (whoever he was) would put this woman (whoever she was) down instead.

'He's the new cleaning boss,' Prune-mouth said, as if reading Connie's thoughts. 'Ooh, I *do* hope Mags doesn't lose her job.' She slotted another biscuit between her lips. Giving a smirk – not an easy thing to do round a Bourbon – she left the room.

Connie stuck out her tongue at the door. Then she bit her lip. *Holy Himalayas, could Mags really get the sack for this?*

She turned round and put her hand in the locker. 'Ignore her, Hue. *She's* the revolting creature.' Connie wished she had a pair of earmuffs for him, to block out insults, like on Bring-Your-Pet-to-School Day. Kate Mullins had *ew-yuck*ed at the sight of him and, a week later, invited only people with furry pets to her party. Even Ciara had made a face the first time she'd seen Hue. Ever since, Connie had kept him hidden away in his cage when she came round, which suited his shyness as much as Ciara's distaste.

Now he was cowering right at the back of the locker, behind all the clutter.

Connie pushed her hand further in. 'Come on,' she murmured. But he was such a tremble of legs and tail and dull brown stress that she couldn't get a grip. He was standing on the front of a piece of paper. The back part was wedged down a gap between the locker and the wall.

Connie took the front edge and pulled it gently towards her, sliding Hue forwards. Now she saw it was a cream-coloured envelope. Grasping the sides like a tray, she lowered it to the floor. She took a little bag from her hoodie pocket and laid three dandelion leaves on the carpet. 'Look, Huey, lovely snack.' Slowly he walked off the envelope to nibble his way back to colour.

Connie frowned. There was an address on the envelope.

Connie Fuller
c/o Mags O'Brien
Dublin Airport
Ireland

Mags must have forgotten to pass it on to her. She couldn't make out the date on the postmark. Turning the envelope over, she opened it. There was a card inside.

Her heart jolted. It was a picture of a chameleon balancing across two vertical sticks that made the number eleven. 'Happy Birthday' was written across the top. She opened the card. Inside were the words:

Happy birthday, Connie

There was a folded sheet of paper tucked in there too.

She sat on the floor, crossed her legs and spread out the paper. A letter. Beneath the printed header and address, it was written by hand.

MEXEL MANN SOLUTIONS
12–14 Merton Street
Leeds LS2 8JH
Ph: +44 113 762 9066
Email: research@mexmansol.co.uk
YOUR FUTURE IS OUR PRESENT

February 4th

Dear Connie,

Happy eleventh birthday. I hope you get this letter, at least so you know that I'm wishing you well for this special day, and at most because a reply would be the best thing ever.

Connie's eyes worked faster than her brain.

> I don't know if you've got my other cards. Maybe Mags didn't pass them on. Or maybe you've scrunched them up and used them for basket-ball practice. I wouldn't blame you. I'm so sorry I haven't written a proper letter before. The reasons are complicated, but this year it feels as if you're old enough, and I'm ready, to connect better. Only if you want to, of course. Letters are polite, safe things, crossing seas and waiting patiently in post boxes, not demanding but inviting a reply.
>
> I wish I knew your address. But as usual I'll have to send it via Mags at the airport. I can't find you on the Internet – and even if I could, no sensible girl (which I'm sure you are) would dream of replying online to someone who claims to be her father.

Connie's breath froze in her throat.

> But I really am, Connie, the dad who left you in your ladybird coat, and Hue in his travel box, nearly seven years ago at the airport café.

I've been paying ever since for that moment when I lost my mind. Literally. I still don't understand fully what happened – and what I do know is too difficult to put down on paper. Perhaps one day I'll get to explain properly. Only if you want me to, of course.

If you do choose to write back, maybe you'd tell me a bit about yourself – your hobbies, your friends, your favourite crisps (mine are smoky bacon), what you do on Saturdays. I'm usually at work, like now, as you can see from the headed paper. How boring is that?

I guess I just want to know that you're happy. And that the worst mistake of my life hasn't ruined yours.

Whether you reply to this letter, dear Connie, or even bother to read it, please know that I'll always be

Your ever-loving dad
Ben

4. Would She?

Connie sat very still. Not a finger moved, not a hair; even her heartbeat seemed to be on holiday. Only her eyes worked frantically, reading the letter again. The words danced before her. And slowly, slowly, they sank into her brain.

> ... best thing ever ... the dad who left you .... worst mistake of my life ... ever-loving

And, most mind-blowing of all:

> ... in your ladybird coat, and Hue in his travel box

He must be real; no-one else could know that!

She read it a third time.

> ... my other cards

So there were more! Mags must have kept them all from her. *Why?* Connie brought her hands to her face. And why her *eleventh* birthday? She'd turned *twelve* this February. That meant the letter was a year and five months old. And it hadn't been opened. There must be a good explanation. Honest, reliable, sometimes annoying, always adoring Mags would never hide things from her deliberately. Especially not cards from—

Would she?

Connie felt dizzy, adrift, as if her heart, lungs and stomach had left their moorings and were floating around inside her body. If she couldn't trust Mags, how could she trust the sun to rise or the world to turn? All these years Mags had hinted – without actually saying – that Dad could be dead. 'No-one knows,' she'd always answered when Connie had asked where he was. 'We never heard from him again, or any of his family. You went into emergency care for six months while I applied to foster you. I'm sorry, Con, I'm sure he loved you very much.'

No-one knows? Never heard from him?

'How could she?!' Connie burst out.

She jumped up. Reaching into Mags's locker again, she rummaged at the back. There were no more envelopes. She put her hands on top of her head, as if to stop it from bursting open. 'What should I do, Huey?' But he was too busy with the dandelion leaves to look up.

So she put the letter, card and envelope in her hoodie pocket and did what she always did when she didn't know what else to do and there was something tall nearby that wasn't alive or wobbly or an electricity pylon.

She climbed.

Using the lockers as handholds and steps, she pulled herself up. She sat on top of the stack and dangled her legs. Maybe up here she'd get a better view of things, see more clearly what to do. But, for once, not even height helped. This discovery was so huge it would take time to sink in properly. And until it did, Mags mustn't know that she'd found the letter.

Connie read it a fourth time. She'd got as far as *favourite crisps* when she heard footsteps in the corridor. Oh no, more visitors. She had to replace the envelope so that Mags would suspect nothing. But the letter? After years of wondering if her dad was even alive, no way was she giving *that* up. She slipped it into a back pocket of her jeans. Then she put the card in the envelope and stuck the flap down; the gum was still sticky enough for it to pass as unopened.

Connie jumped down from the lockers as the footsteps stopped outside the door. She shoved the envelope into Mags's locker and wedged it down the back again. Then she spun round and reached down to scoop Hue up from the carpet. But before she could return him to his pouch, the door opened.

Mags walked in, followed by a man. 'There'll be no more trouble,' she was saying. She stopped. 'What the—? Connie, I told you to keep him hidden!' She widened her eyes at Hue. Then she turned to the man, 'Joe, I'm so sorry.'

Joe? The boss who'd 'know what to do', who'd 'put the thing down if he's got any sense'. And now here he was – and here Hue was – and it was all Connie's fault.

5. The Boss

'Back in his pouch.' Mags wagged her finger at Connie. 'Now!'

Beside her, the boss raised his hand. 'No, it's grand. I mean, I'd actually like to see him.'

He didn't *look* like a lizard murderer. Or even a boss, the way he was smiling – to be honest, a bit stupidly. His hair was brown and wispy, like a lawn in a heatwave. He stooped slightly as if trying to take up less space. But most un-bosslike was the way he looked at Mags.

Connie's second favourite animal after Hue was Ciara's spaniel, Flummox. (Ciara had been invited to Kate Mullins's Furry-Pets-Only Party but declined out of loyalty to Connie.) And it was Flummox who came to mind when she saw Joe's eyes. They were shiny and soft: even shinier and softer when Mags spoke to him.

'Fine by me,' Mags said, in a very different tone from the one she'd used with Connie: light and high, as if her voice were fluttering its eyelashes. 'Go ahead, Joe.'

Did people always use their boss's first name before being sacked?

Joe almost crept towards Hue. 'Never seen a real live chameleon. Do they really change col— *aaah!*'

You'd think Hue had understood, the way his blue stripes swaggered into turquoise and his legs showed off in pink.

'All OK here, Con?' Mags said cheerily, now that she saw Hue was a hit. 'You're not too bored?'

Well, I was a bit at first but then GUESS WHAT? I found a letter from my DAD that you've already opened and kept HIDDEN for nearly EIGHTEEN MONTHS even though you've been telling me for EIGHT YEARS that you don't know where he is, or if he's even STILL ALIVE.

'Yeah,' was what Connie actually said. Swallowing the storm in her throat, she turned away and crouched on the floor to gather up the rags of dandelion leaves. Her thoughts were a swirl; she mustn't let them spill on to her face.

'Did anyone come in?' said Mags.

'A lady. But I kept Hue in his pouch,' Connie lied. *A pretty small lie compared to SOME around here.* 'She didn't seem a fan of yours.'

Mags sniffed. 'Purple hair?'

Connie nodded at the floor.

'Sue. I bet she knew all about Hue escaping.'

'Mm.' Connie had run out of actual words.

'I'm sure she was thrilled I was in trouble.'

'You're not,' said Joe. 'I've had a word with management. It's not like this fella could do any harm.' He bent over Hue and stretched out a finger to stroke him.

'No!' Connie said, finding her words now that Hue was at risk. 'I mean, sorry, but he doesn't like being touched by strangers. Or even me, sometimes. See, he's gone dull.' Hue was turning the same brown as the carpet. 'That means he's scared.'

'Oh, right.' Joe backed away. 'I thought their colours changed for camouflage.'

'A bit. But mostly because of feelings or temperature. Greys and browns when he's upset or cold, and brighter when he's happy and warm.' Good job *her* feelings didn't show like that; right now she'd be the colour of dirty dishwater.

Joe whistled. 'Clever little guy, aren't you?' Now that he'd retreated, calm blue-green stripes reappeared on Hue's back. 'What a showman. I'd like a pet like that meself. More interesting than Mr Spickles.'

'Who?' said Mags.

'My hedgehog. Well, not exactly *mine*, but he likes to visit the garden.' He smiled sheepishly. Connie pictured him sitting on his sofa with a ready-meal and Mr Spickles beside him, watching *Fair City* or some other soap that was so packed with drama you didn't need any in real life. She decided she liked Joe.

'Anyway,' Mags said, 'time to go, Connie.'

Still unable to look at her, Connie bent over Hue. She put her hand on the ground, palm up, so that he could crawl on top. She lifted him slowly, brought the pouch out from her hoodie and lowered him inside.

'Hasn't he got a cage?' said Joe. 'Or a tank, or whatever chameleons have?'

'A travel box,' said Mags, 'yes. But Connie smuggled him in today. She knew he wouldn't be allowed.'

'Well, now.' Joe fiddled his fingers together. 'I wouldn't say that. I mean, as long as he stays in his box, I don't see why you can't bring him in. Bit of company, like.' He gave what Connie guessed was meant to be a wink but looked more as if a fly had crashed into his eye. 'Might not want to advertise it, though.'

She got the feeling that even if rules weren't actually being broken, they were being twisted like spaghetti for her, or rather for Mags.

— · —

They caught the lift down to the ground floor. Crossing the Arrivals area to the exit, Connie lagged behind, letting Joe talk to Mags so that she didn't have to. As she passed the Pie in the Sky café, a girl sitting at a table held up her phone camera. She clicked it. Connie glared at her. If there was one thing she hated more than crowds, it was having her photo taken. The girl raised a hand and smiled faintly. She wore a red baseball cap. She looked about sixteen.

'Hey!' A boy sitting beside her, who looked around Connie's age, grabbed the phone from the girl's hand.

'You can't just ...' *They must be brother and sister,* Connie thought.

Two grown-ups sat opposite. The lady was writing on a laptop and didn't notice the drama.

But the man leaned across the café table. 'Delete that, Abri. Now.'

The girl snatched the phone back from the boy. Sulkily she pressed the phone. The boy looked over at Connie and grinned.

It was such a wonky, friendly smile that Connie felt her lips parting too.

Then she turned and fled after Mags.

6. The Think Pad

Back at home, Connie refused Mags's offer to make her lunch. Instead she threw together a peanut butter sandwich and took it upstairs. In her bedroom she went to Hue's terrarium, a tall cage with wire mesh walls that stood against the far wall. The inside was crowded with leafy branches. Putting the sandwich on the floor, she opened the cage door. She lifted Hue out of his pouch and set him on a branch inside.

'What do I do about the letter, Huey?'

He raised his head. On the branch above, a cricket sat composing an opera, or painting its toenails, or whatever crickets do all day. There was a flash, a flicker, and the creature was gone, reeled in on Hue's tongue. The cricket crumpled like a leaf as the chameleon crunched and swallowed it, his throat bulging.

'Thanks for your help,' Connie muttered.

She looked round the room. She'd designed it herself and, for her tenth birthday, Mags had worked overtime to pay for the revamp. There were knobs and grooves all over the walls, connected by lines that Connie had drawn in marker pen, like a giant dot-to-dot. Each line marked a different climbing route up to her bed in the loft, and each was named after a famous expedition up Mount Everest.

The idea had come from Hue. For as long as she could remember, Connie had watched him climb – up and down, the right way up or upside down – scaling anything from branches to chair legs to the mesh of the terrarium. How she admired his careful confidence as he grasped with his pincer hands or hung by his elegant tail. As she'd grown older, and Mags's love had seemed to close around her like a tightening belt, she'd started to envy Hue's climbing, and copy it too. It was wonderful to rise above the 'Carefuls' and 'Don't go fars' of life on the ground and to hide up high, out of Mags's anxious sight. Even more anxious after Connie had slipped on a rock at the beach and sprained her ankle three years ago. They hadn't been back to the beach since. Connie's protests had led to the room renovation, even though Mags had inherited the little house and every part of it held precious memories of her beloved parents.

Now Connie chose the American West Ridge, first climbed on Everest in 1963. The long and tricky route began by the bedroom door, crossed the left-hand wall then turned up steeply to the opening into the loft. There were only three foot-grooves and two handholds on the way.

Clamping the sandwich between her teeth, Connie wedged the toe of her trainer into the first groove. She raised her arm and grasped the first handhold. Up and along the wall she climbed, from knob to groove, until she reached the loft opening. She pulled herself through, twisted round and sat on the bed. She ate her sandwich, then lay back and stared at the sloping ceiling.

This was her think pad – not the slinky computer she wasn't allowed to have, but the place where she came to work things out: long division; what to get Mags for her birthday; how to stop Kate Mullins telling the whole class that she and her family had seen Mags at the airport cleaning toilets on their way to Marbella. Perhaps the air was clearer, or perhaps the height focused

Connie's mind. Whatever the reason, she usually found answers up here.

She took the letter from her pocket. Spreading it out on her lap, she reread it. And sure enough, her plan became clear.

If Mags had lied for all these years, why would she tell the truth if Connie asked now? No, better to say nothing and do her own investigations, at least for the moment. She had what she needed: an address, an email and a phone number.

She leaned towards the loft opening and called down, 'We must proceed with caution, Hue.' That sounded professional, like on police shows. Hue could be her sidekick. Didn't all the best detectives work in pairs: Holmes and Watson, Cagney and Lacey? 'Connie and Cham,' she said. 'We'll google the place where he works first, see if there's a photo or anything about him on the website.'

Down in his cage, Hue didn't look too keen. He proceeded with his own caution into the undergrowth. Connie sighed. Googling was all very well. But how, when she didn't have a computer?

— · —

'Can I use your phone?' she asked at dinner.

Mags speared a sausage. 'What for?'

'To call Ciara.'

Mags's fork stopped in mid-air. 'I thought you said she was flying to Spain tonight. She won't have reception on the plane.'

Holy Himalayas. Connie had forgotten she'd told Mags that. 'Well, just to look something up, then. Quickly.'

Mags frowned. Even her fork looked suspicious. 'Only for homework, love, that's the rule.'

Connie raked lines in her mashed potato. *Now what?* She couldn't ask Mags again. If only she had her own phone.

A line from the letter leapt into her brain. Something about her dad not being able to find her on the Internet. Connie dropped her fork. Could *that* be why she wasn't allowed a phone or computer? Was Mags scared that someone – like a living dad, for instance – might be able to track her down?

She couldn't sit here a minute longer. 'Got a head-ache,' she mumbled. 'I'm going to my room.' She pushed her chair back.

'Are you OK, love? Do you want a paracetamol? A drink? Anything else I can get you?'

How about a nice hot cup of truth? Connie fumed silently, marching upstairs.

In her bedroom, she went to Hue's terrarium. He was hidden in the foliage.

'How can I get on the Internet, Huey?' she said, pressing her palm against the mesh.

A blue–green bottom poked out between two leaves. A red tail rose in the air. A gleaming blob dropped on to the newspaper lining the floor of the cage.

Connie opened the door again. She took the edges of the paper, lifted it out and folded it in half. Taking a clean sheet of newspaper from a pile she kept by the wall, she spread it on the floor of the cage.

And there was her answer. Cleaning.

'Thanks for your help,' she said to the red tail that was wriggling back into the undergrowth. And this time she meant it.

7. A Fly and a Lie

Connie made her offer in the car the next morning. It was the longest sentence she'd spoken to Mags since finding the letter.

'What a kind thought!' said Mags, smiling in the rear-view mirror.

Connie stared out of the window to hide how kind it wasn't.

'We'll ask Joe,' Mags continued. 'I'm sure he'll be delighted.'

And he was, in his shy and drooping way, when they met him by the lift in the Arrivals hall. 'Thanks, Connie,' he said, though it was Mags he was looking at. 'Now you mention it, my office could do with a clean.' He nodded at the travel box she was carrying. 'You can let himself out in my room. It's messy enough. Disneyland for a lizard,

I'd say. Mum's the word, though.' He did his crashed-fly wink at Mags.

Entering Joe's office on the fourth floor, Connie gave a silent whoop. Because there on his desk, just as she'd hoped, was a computer.

Mags fetched a Hoover, a bottle of cleaning spray and a cloth. 'When you've finished, go down to the café,' she said. 'I'll meet you there after my shift.'

'Funny thing,' Joe said, looking round. 'Head of cleaning and look at my own room.' He scratched his forehead as if he didn't have a clue how the clutter of dirty cups and papers could have got there.

When he and Mags had left, Connie put Hue's box on the desk. She unclipped the lid and lifted him out. 'No pooping,' she said, as he crept gingerly between the papers like a skater testing an icy pond. She sat at the desk and took out the letter from her pocket.

She swallowed. *The moment before the rest of my life.*

'Right.' She laced her fingers. 'Detective time, Hue.'

She found the mouse and clicked it. The screensaver flashed on, a photo of a hedgehog. That must be Joe's garden visitor. With its furry face and manky bristles, it was cute *and* yucky, all at the same time. That would confuse Kate Mullins and her Furry-Pets-Only party.

Connie clicked the login box. 'Oh no.' The password. She hadn't thought of that. She typed 'Joe.'

Incorrect password, it said under the box.

She didn't know Joe's surname. So she tried 'Airport.' Wrong again. She stared at the screen. What had Joe called that hedgehog again? She typed 'Mr Spickles.'

You're locked out, it said on the screen.

'Dammit!' she muttered, shoving the mouse away. 'Now what, Hue?'

He offered a pretty but unhelpful suggestion of blue and yellow stripes, then climbed into a little pot of pens.

Connie sighed. She'd have to find another way. Meanwhile, better get cleaning.

A fly buzzed in through the window. It landed on a filing cabinet in the corner, then took off again. Hue froze on top of the pot like a crazy piece of stationery, his tail curled round a pen. Only his eyes moved, following the fly as it danced through the air, as if to music no-one else could hear.

Beneath a jumble of folders on the desk, Connie found a heart-shaped box of chocolates. A Post-it note was stuck on top.

TO MAGS.

FROM ~~JOE~~. AN ADMIRER

Despite her anger at Mags, Connie smiled. She imagined Joe buying the box days ago and still waiting for the courage to give it.

'Helloo-hoo,' sang a voice. 'Only mee-hee.'

Connie pushed the pen-holder, with Hue still on top, behind the computer.

The door opened.

'You again!' Prune-mouth Sue stood in the doorway. 'What are you doing here?' Her voice had gone from fairy godmother to wicked queen. 'Where's Joe?'

'He asked me to clean his office.'

Sue marched into the room and put her hands on her hips. 'And to nick his chocolates, I see.'

Connie looked at the box in her hand. 'No. They're for my ...' Somehow she couldn't say 'foster mum' to this woman. 'For Mags.'

Sue's mouth fell open. Connie couldn't help hoping that the fly would buzz inside. But no, it landed on Sue's sleeve as she stared at the box. 'Oh,' she said in a tiny voice, a million miles from the fluty toot outside the door. 'Well then, you'd better get on with – *aaagh!*'

Like a streak of sticky lightning, Hue's tongue shot all the way out and snatched the fly from Sue's arm. She stumbled backwards. Hue pottered round the front of the computer, his red throat pulsing as he munched.

'That.' Sue whipped a hanky from her pocket. 'Disgusting.' She rubbed her sleeve madly. 'Thing.' She jabbed a finger at Connie. 'I can't believe you brought him in again. Wait till Joe hears about—'

'He said I could.' Connie cut in.

'You little liar. As if he'd—'

'Because he really likes Mags.' The words spilled out like pins from a box, stabbing into Sue. Her bony shoulders twitched.

'And he likes Hue too.'

Sue glared at the chameleon. He crunched the last morsel of fly with what could only be called a smirk.

'Well,' she said at last. 'You just ... you just ...' She pointed at the box in Connie's hands. 'You just tell Joe that you found those chocolates and the note. And you tell him that Mags doesn't like *him*, so he should back off. Otherwise ...' She blinked furiously. 'Otherwise I'll go to his boss and tell him how ...' She held out a hand towards Hue. 'Ow!' She clasped it theatrically with her other hand. 'How that thing *bit* me.' She fixed Connie with small grey eyes, like nails hammered into her face. 'Ooh, I wonder who Mr Ryan will believe. A staff member who's worked here for five loyal years, or a girl who smuggled in a revolting reptile that caused chaos in Arrivals?' Sue opened the door. 'And there's no fooling me. I'll be watching Mags and Joe, so I'll know if you've done it.' She left, slamming the door behind her.

Connie let out a long, slow breath. *So Sue likes Joe, who likes Mags, who likes Joe, which is why Sue doesn't like Mags, and why she doesn't like me either, so she takes it out on Hue.* Grown-ups. All those years to practise and still they behaved like kids. But, childish or not,

Sue could cause huge trouble if she claimed Hue had bitten her. Huge, put-downy kind of trouble.

'They'll have to put *me* down first!' Connie muttered. Plus, Mags had lied to her big time. Here was a chance to return the compliment.

8. Cowpats

Of course Mags deserved it, but Connie couldn't bring herself to lie to Joe's face. He'd been so kind, she didn't want to see his look of hurt. So when she'd finished cleaning, she took a scrap of paper from the desk and a pen from the holder.

I found these chocolates on the desk and I couldn't help reading the note. Sorry but Mags has got a ~~boy~~man-friend.

From Connie

Putting it on top of the box, she felt a bit bad. Just a bit. Not very. Honest.

She took the lift down to the Arrivals hall and went to the Pie in the Sky café. There was still an hour before Mags finished. Connie sat at the table behind the pillar again, hoping she'd be hidden from the café man's disapproving looks after Hue's performance yesterday.

Fat chance. Mags must have told Dave to look out for her because he came over immediately. 'Joe warned me you'd be back, you and your pal. That lid better be on tight.'

Connie smiled in what she hoped was a reassuring way. *Maybe* he'll *lend me his phone.* But the look on Dave's face sent that idea straight to bed without any supper.

When he'd gone, Connie scanned the Arrivals hall for other potential phone lenders. An elderly couple who looked lendy but not phone-owny. A mum trying to soothe a wailing baby; her hands weren't free to fish out a phone. A lady in a suit rushing for the exit – too busy. Oh dear, there was no-one. Except ...

That girl! The one from yesterday who'd taken Connie's photo. There she was again, wafting round the Arrivals hall with her phone in one hand and a little bag in the other. She wore a long red floaty skirt and eye-shadow the colour of Granny Smith apples. Connie shifted her chair so that she could see past the pillar. There, across the café, were the girl's brother and parents too, sitting at the same table as yesterday. *Strange*, she thought. Their second day in Arrivals. Had they met someone off the plane yesterday and come to meet someone else today? Or had yesterday's arrival been delayed a whole day?

Well, whatever the reason, that girl owed her a favour. Pushing her chair back, Connie stood up. But something about the girl – the straight back, the loud make-up and most of all that wafting, so graceful and self-assured – made her sit down again.

She fingered the letter in her pocket. *Come on. She's your best chance.*

Standing up again, Connie took a step towards the girl. But now she was wafting away towards the loos. She went into the toilet for disabled people. Connie frowned. Was wafting a disability?

Returning to her table, she sat down and leaned towards Hue's box. 'We'll wait for someone who's got a phone *and* a lendy face,' she murmured through the airholes in the lid.

'Hi.'

Connie looked up, startled.

The girl's brother was standing by her chair. 'I saw you looking at my sister like you wanted to talk to her. My dad said I should come and say sorry she took your photo yesterday. It was nothing personal. I mean, she's been taking photos of loads of people in the airport.' There was English in his accent, and something else too, soft but strong; his 'dad' was more like 'ded' and his 't's meant business.

'Oh,' Connie mumbled, 'well, thanks.' Why was her face heating up?

'*Did* you want to talk to her? I wouldn't bother.' He gave his wonky grin.

'I, well ...' Why was her tongue icing over?

'My name's Thyo, by the way. Like Theo, but with a y.'

'Y,' Connie echoed stupidly.

'Because it's short for Ichthyosaurus.'

'No, I didn't mean *why*. I meant – *what*?'

'You know, the dinosaur fish. What's yours?'

She was still staring at him in amazement as she answered, 'Connie.'

He laughed. 'That's funny. Makes me think of old-fashioned maids in frilly caps.'

Indignation thawed her tongue. 'Well, Ichthyosaurus is hardly *un*-funny.'

'Oh, don't be offended.' His grin widened. 'My ma says taking offence is like seeing a cowpat flying towards you and just standing there.'

Before Connie could ask how a cowpat could fly, he said, 'I mean, maybe someone threw it at you deliberately – but you can still move away to stop it landing on you.'

Before Connie could ask why someone would be throwing cowpats at all, he went on, 'Though I wasn't throwing a cowpat because I think funny and old-fashioned are good things for a name to be.'

Before she could decide whether to take his advice and not be offended, he went on, 'And if *I* hadn't moved out of the way of all the cowpats that have been thrown at *me*, you'd be talking to a massive great poop hill.'

Connie couldn't help smiling. Thyo took that as an invitation. Grinning his face off, he pulled out a chair.

'Why are you here two days in a row?' he said, sitting down opposite her.

'Why are *you*?'

'I asked first,' Thyo said, still smiling.

'Uh, OK. I come in the mornings because my ... um ... friend works here.' Connie felt a stab of guilt. But no way was she telling this strange, confident boy that she didn't have a real mum, only a foster parent who worked at the airport. 'Your turn,' she said. Behind Thyo, she saw his sister come out of the toilet and drift towards them.

'Well,' he began, 'we're coming here to – ow!' Something hit the back of his head. He bent down and picked up a tube of toothpaste, still grinning his unoffendable grin. 'To wash.'

9. Fossils and Fainting

Thyo with a y produced a toothbrush from his pocket. 'We're staying on a campsite,' he said. 'The water's not working in the bathroom block. I don't see why we can't just wash in the sea, but Her Royal Sisterness says the salt's too strong for her perfect skin. So our ma thought of coming to the airport until it's fixed.'

So *that* was why his sister had gone to the toilet for disabled people. It had its own private sink.

Thyo reached his arm across the table. 'What's in there?' He patted Hue's box.

'Don't!' Connie flicked his hand away. 'He can feel everything.'

'He? A pet?' Thyo leaned forward and peered through the slits in the lid. 'I can only see leaves.'

Connie laid a protective hand on the box. 'He's hiding.'

'Who is?'

'A chameleon.'

Thyo's eyes filled his face. 'Deadly!'

'No. But he can bite.'

Thyo laughed. 'Can you take him out?'

Connie glanced at the café counter. Dave stood behind it, frowning in their direction. She was about to say she wasn't allowed to remove Hue, when a thought struck her.

'Have you got a phone?'

Thyo nodded.

'I'll let you see him if I can borrow it.'

'Deal.'

Connie looked at Dave again. He'd turned away to serve a customer. She put Hue's box on the floor so that it was hidden by the table. Thyo came round and sat beside her.

'Don't make a fuss,' she murmured, bending forward and unclipping the lid. Hue's blue head poked out between the leaves. 'And not too close. He doesn't like strangers.'

But he did like showing off. Hue crept out from the leaves, flaunting blue and green stripes. His head turned purple like a luminous bruise.

'Wow. My ma would love him.' Thyo pointed across the café. The man and woman from yesterday were sitting at the same table. 'She's mad on reptiles. Well, dead ones. She's a palaeontologist.'

Connie had always thought of fossil hunters as old men with beards and dirty fingernails, nothing like this glamorous woman sharing a scone with Thyo's dad. Catching Connie's eye, the woman smiled and wriggled her hand in a little wave. She had a cloud of black hair and big dangly earrings.

Connie wriggle-waved back and felt an awkward sort of nice. 'So are you on holiday here?'

'Yes and no,' said Thyo. 'I mean it's school holidays for me and Abri. But Ma's come to look at a fossil. We're here for a month.'

Connie remembered the fossils they'd drawn on a school visit to the Natural History Museum. The squiggly stones were tiny and grey with impossible Latin names. She couldn't think of a duller way to spend a minute, let alone a month.

Until Thyo said, 'It's part of a dinosaur skeleton.'

OK, *now* he was talking. When Billy Kerr had drawn a T-rex eating a Stegosaurus, instead of sketching a boring old lump of coral, the museum guide had sniffed and said, 'Dream on, lad. Only two dinosaur bones have ever been found in Ireland.'

'The geologists here don't know the species,' said Thyo, 'but they know the age from the rocks around it. They've asked Ma to come and identify it because she's an expert on the Early Jurassic.'

'The what?' The only Jurassics Connie had heard of were Park and World.

'The time when this unknown dinosaur lived, about a hundred and ninety-five million years ago. That's when Ichthyosaurs were around too. Ma once found a whole skeleton in Germany.'

'And named you after it? What a compliment!'

He nodded so proudly that Connie felt bad for poking fun. He pointed to his sister who'd returned to their parents' table. 'And she's Abri, after Abrictosaurus. Ma found one in South Africa.'

'Is that where you're from?' said Connie.

Thyo laughed. 'I was waiting for that. People here always ask where I come from when they first meet me. Sometimes they actually want to know. But other times they're just saying, "You're obviously not from *here*, so what are you *doing* here?"'

Connie felt her cheeks burn. 'I actually want to know. Really.'

He waved a hand. 'It's fine. Even if you didn't, I'm good at dodging cowpats, remember? We have a house in South Africa. It's where Ma was born. Dad's from England so we go there and stay with my grandparents too. He's an artist. He doesn't sell many paintings, but the good thing is he can do it anywhere, so we travel all over for Ma's work.'

Connie pictured beaches and deserts and jungles, and most of all mountains that tickled the clouds. She felt restless and fluttery, as if a bird were trapped in her chest. 'Lucky you. I never go anywhere.'

Thyo scrunched his nose. 'You think? I mean it's good seeing different places and stuff. But her projects take a few months at most, then we move on. I've changed school seven times in four years. There's no point trying to make friends.'

Connie hadn't thought of that. She'd been best friends with Ciara since Junior Infants. Ciara was going to Glenview College in September, which Mags couldn't afford. Connie dreaded the thought of St Peter's without Ciara. Lately she'd been having nightmares about walking into class on the first day and dissolving into a puddle on the floor in front of all the staring faces.

'People don't bother,' said Thyo, 'when they know I'm not staying. Which I guess makes sense.'

Making sense doesn't make it right, Connie thought, feeling suddenly sorry for him. He looked anything but sorry for himself, though, so she just nodded.

'What I *would* like,' he said, 'is to be in one place long enough to grow things. To have my own garden.' As if to start the process, he reached over and broke a twig off Hue's branch.

'Hey, don't do that,' said Connie. 'You'll scare him.'

'Scare who?' said a voice behind her. She turned to see Thyo's dad approaching.

'Don't let me interrupt,' he said. 'We just wondered if you two would like a scone.' He held out a hand to Connie. 'Hi, I'm Ned.'

She wasn't used to grown-ups shaking her hand, let alone introducing themselves by their first names. 'Connie,' she mumbled, brushing his fingers shyly.

Thyo's dad was tall and skinny and looked as if he didn't quite fit together. His legs were too long for his body and his head was too big for his neck. His ears stuck out and his fair hair was tied back in a pony tail. He reminded Connie of a foal standing up for the first time.

'So who's this scared chap?' He bent towards the box.

'No, Dad,' said Thyo, jumping up from his chair. 'Don't.'

'Ma and I have been wondering what you're looking a—*aahh!*' Ned stepped back. '*Oaahh.*' There was a sigh. Then a thud. Then a crash.

Ned lay on the floor beside an upturned chair. Thyo bent over him. His mum and sister ran up. Connie clipped on the lid of Hue's box and slid the whole thing under the table to shelter Hue from the commotion.

'Ned?' Thyo's mum crouched by his side. 'You OK? What happened?'

He sat up. 'I think I ...' He rubbed his head. 'Fainted. That.' He waved vaguely towards Hue's box, now firmly closed.

'I tried to tell you,' said Thyo. He stood up and turned to Connie. 'My dad's a herpetophobe.'

She blinked at him.

'He's scared of reptiles.'

'You're joking,' she said. But for once there was no wonky smile. 'Is that a thing?'

Ned's groan was her answer.

Dave hurried over. 'What's going on?'

'Could you get him some water, please?' Connie said quickly, before anyone could explain and get Hue into trouble again. As Dave headed off, Thyo's mum helped Ned to his feet.

'So your mum's into dinosaurs,' Connie murmured to Thyo, 'which were the biggest-ever reptiles, and your dad can't stand even little ones? Weird.'

Thyo swept out his arm. 'Welcome to my family.'

His mum smiled at Connie. 'Ned just told me who's in the box. I'd love to meet him.'

Him? Connie liked her already.

'But not now. We need to get this guy home.' She nodded towards her husband. 'I'm Naledi, by the way. Thanks for entertaining my boy.' Her voice was rich and warm, like the sound of sunshine. She took one of Ned's arms. Abri took the other.

'Come on, Thyo,' Naledi said over her shoulder. He turned to go.

'Hey, no. I mean, what about your phone?' said Connie

He stopped. 'Didn't you say you come here in the mornings? We'll be here again tomorrow too. I promise you can use it then.' He followed his family to the exit and waved as they went through the doors.

Dave returned. 'Customers,' he muttered, plonking the glass of water on the table. 'You couldn't invent 'em.'

10. Joe's Cold Shoulder

The funny thing was, Connie felt a kind of relief that she hadn't used Thyo's phone. Of course she wanted to find out about her dad's work. But to be honest, Mexel Mann Solutions sounded a bit dull: the sort of place that made parts for computers or did research into cardboard. Holy Himalayas, was her dad a cardboard researcher? Or even worse, a cardboard *technician* (which was one of those words people used when they didn't understand what the job really was)? Did he sit at a conveyor belt all day long, folding along dotted lines to make boxes for teabags? Even if Mexel Mann made exciting things like robots that did the washing up, or pens that could spell, it meant that he didn't do any of the other jobs she'd dreamed about over the years. He wasn't an actor like Brad Pitt, or a lawyer who defended the rights of orang-utans, or a street artist like Banksy. Worst of all, he wasn't Chris Sharma, her favourite climber.

Perhaps there was a clue in his handwriting. When Thyo's family had gone, Connie returned to her table. Putting Hue's box on top, she sat down and took out her dad's letter. She was examining the hook of the gs and curve of the cs for signs of cardboard-researching when she caught sight of Mags heading across the Arrivals hall. Connie stuffed the letter into her pocket. She took out her notebook and pen and got busy doodling.

'That's me done,' said Mags, arriving at the table. 'Were you waiting long, love?'

'No.' Connie closed her notebook.

'How was the cleaning? I hope Hue behaved himself.'

'Yup.' Thank goodness Mags hadn't appeared ten minutes earlier.

'Right so, let's go.' Mags turned. 'Oh.' Her hand flew to her hair. 'Hello Joe.'

He was walking towards them, head down. 'Thanks for cleaning,' he mumbled to Connie, and hurried on.

Mags frowned. 'Everything OK, Joe?'

'It's Mr Dooley,' he said, without looking round.

Mags blinked after him. 'What's he upset about?'

You, Connie answered silently. *Or rather your man-friend. And it serves you right. A lie for a lie.*

Driving home, Mags gripped the steering wheel with both hands. 'You saw him this morning, nice as noodles. What did I do?'

Connie shrugged. She leaned forward from the back seat and turned on the radio to end the conversation.

— · —

'Fancy asking *me,*' she said later in her bedroom, putting Hue back in his cage. 'As if I'm her agony aunt. Honestly, Huey, grown-ups are ridiculous.'

He looked at her as if to say, 'You'll be one soon enough,' and disappeared into the foliage.

She climbed the South Col route (1953) to her bed. It was an easy ascent up the right-hand wall, with five footholds and four handholds, between posters of her favourite mountains. Sitting on her bed, she looked out of the window on her left.

Mags was crossing the lawn of their little garden. She stopped at the vegetable patch and bent over. Connie couldn't see much beyond her bottom, but knew she was at her daily ritual of weeding. You'd almost feel sorry for the dandelions, the way she yanked them up and hurled them on to the lawn. Little tufts sailed up from their Einstein heads. Mags stood up and rubbed her back. Then she bent over again and pulled up a lettuce.

Connie remembered what Thyo had said about wanting to stay somewhere long enough to grow things. That was exactly what bored her about gardening: everything took so long. But as Mags threw the lettuce on to the lawn, Connie felt a grudging flicker of gratitude. She had all the time in the world to watch things grow.

Mags wiped her hands on her trousers. She sat on the lawn with her legs straight out in front. The top of her head looked soft and sad, with curls that wriggled in all directions, as if unsure where to go.

Stop it, Connie told herself. *She was sure enough when she hid Dad's letter from me. Why should I feel sorry for her? She deserved that note to Joe. What's a ruined romance compared to an eight-year lie?*

She turned away from the window. She had every right to find out about her dad. She'd borrow Thyo's phone tomorrow, pretend she was looking up famous climbers or something, and google Mexel Mann. That was it. Simple pimple. No harm done. It was her secret; she wouldn't tell a soul.

11. Your Future Is Our Present

'Eight years? You haven't seen him for *eight years*?!' Thyo leaned across the café table next morning. His face was all eyes.

How on earth did that happen? Connie pressed a fist to her mouth. So much for not telling a soul. Something about the way Thyo had bounded up to her when he arrived with his family, grinning his head off, had made it impossible to lie. Her story had tumbled out, from the ladybird coat and the marshmallow worms to Mags becoming her foster mum. And telling it felt good, as if she could breathe properly for the first time in two days.

'How could he do that?' Thyo shook his head. 'Just walk away. I mean, he was your *dad*!'

'Is.' She told him about the letter that Mags had hidden.

His eyebrows flew up. 'How could *she* do that?'

Connie felt a punch of satisfaction. If outrage was a person, it would be Thyo with his wide eyes and fists bunched on the table. She moved Hue's box to block the view from Dave's counter. Then she brought out the letter from her pocket and smoothed it out in front of him.

Thyo read it. 'Wow,' he murmured, and read it again. 'Wowowow.' He leaned back in his seat and let out a whistly breath. Then he took his phone from his pocket and pushed it across the table. 'Google away.'

Connie pushed it back. 'You do it. I'm not used to smartphones.' She spelt it out. 'M-E-X-E-L.' He pressed in the letters. 'M-A-N-N.'

Google came up with a single website. Thyo clicked on it. They waited an endless three seconds.

MEXEL MANN SOLUTIONS

Your Future Is Our Present

At MMS we offer sustainable answers to the world's greatest problems in science, technology and health. We are global leaders in cutting-edge innovation, long-term development and resource planning. Our pioneering methods build on past success for future prosperity.

'I don't understand a word,' Connie said. 'I mean, I understand the *actual* words, but not when they're put together.'

'Mmm.' Thyo frowned. 'It's all technical-speak. If Ma was here, we could ask her.'

'No.' Connie looked across the café to what seemed to have become Thyo's family's table, where his dad was now reading the paper. 'I don't want anyone else to know, not yet. Where *is* your mum? And your sister?'

'Abri's gone to wash, though I don't know why she bothers because she'll just cake her face in make-up afterwards. Ma's at a meeting with a film director.' Thyo said it so casually you'd think it was a dentist's appointment. 'He wants to make a documentary about her digging up the fossil or something.'

'That's amazing!' said Connie, as impressed as he wasn't.

'Yeah, whatever.' He held out the phone. 'Anyway, go ahead and call your dad.'

'What? No.' Connie twisted her hands in her lap. 'I mean, I just want to find out about him, not *contact* him. Not yet, anyway. What would I say? "Hi Dad, how've you been for the last eight years?"'

'Oh.' Thyo chewed his lip. 'I see what you mean.' He pointed to the letter on the table. 'Maybe email him instead?'

Connie swallowed. 'Email him?' Seriously, did Thyo have any idea how hard this was for her?

He read the letter again. Then he tapped his phone, sticking his tongue between his teeth in concentration. 'How about something like this?'

```
Thyo Miles <Thyomiles@gmail.com>
To research@mexmansol.co.uk


Dear Dad,

I only just got the letter you sent
nearly a year and a half ago because
Mags hid it. I'd love to hear from you
```

again. I don't have a phone but you can
reply to this email and Thyo will pass
it on. He's the best.

Love Connie

She couldn't help grinning. 'Well, I'd put Dear Mr Fuller instead of Dad. And I'd take out the bit about Mags hiding his letter, because it might put him off if he knows I'm going behind her back. And *definitely* cut out "He's the best." That's for me to decide.'

'Trust me.' Thyo bowed in his seat. 'You will.'

'But apart from that, I suppose it's the kind of thing I'd – oh.' Connie snatched the letter away as Thyo's sister floated up. She wore green shorts, a stripy pink and purple T-shirt and a yellow beret. Clashing and crazy, she looked brilliant.

'Wash time, stinko.' She handed the toothpaste to Thyo.

'Hi,' she said, smiling vaguely at Connie. 'So my brother says you've got a chameleon.' She pointed to Hue's box. 'Can I take a photo for my portfolio?'

'Well ...' As Connie tried to look as if she knew what a portfolio was, Thyo held up his phone. 'I rewrote it. Better?'

'I guess so,' she said. 'I mean, if I ever did decide to email him, that would be the sort of—'

'If?' Thyo stood up. 'I just did.'

12. Actually over Jupiter

'You WHAT?' Connie tried to grab the phone. But Thyo whisked it behind his back and took the toothpaste from the table.

'Gotta clean my teeth,' he said, and rushed off.

'Ooh.' Abri sat down at the table, her eyes alight beneath her silver-mascara'd eyelashes. 'What's my sad little bro done now?'

'He – uh, nothing.' Connie death-glared Thyo's back as he headed towards the toilet door.

'Mind if I ...?' And before Connie could protest, Abri had whipped out her phone from the pocket of her shorts and clicked it. 'Your face! You look as if you've just been dumped by your boyfriend.'

Connie felt her cheeks catch fire. 'What?'

Abri laughed. 'I know. Who'd go out with Thyo? But it's perfect for my project.' She paused.

Connie knew she was supposed to ask, 'What project?' So she didn't.

Abri told her anyway. 'I want to be a photographer. I'm applying for a course and I need to do a portfolio over the summer.'

Ah. So *portfolio* was a fancy word for a bunch of photos taken without people's permission.

'I'm taking pictures round the airport. The idea is that you look at a photo and work out the story behind it. Like this one.' Abri held up her phone. 'Maybe it *was* your boyfriend dumping you, or maybe you just drank some sour milk, or maybe someone ran off with your purse. Everyone comes up with their own version.'

Connie winced at the sight of her furious face. 'But those are all the *wrong* stories. He's *not* my boyfriend, and I haven't drunk anything, and my purse is in my pocket.'

'That's the point,' said Abri. 'We decide stuff all the time just by looking at people. How old they are, what their house is like, if they're nice or whatever, depending on their face or their coat or the way they eat a sandwich. And we can be so wrong. Like maybe you thought I was a bad person two days ago because I took your photo without asking.'

Connie opened her mouth. But before she could think of a polite yet honest answer, Abri went on, 'When actually I'm a fantastically brilliant person who took it for noble, artistic reasons you had no idea about.'

Connie closed her mouth.

'Or maybe you thought, who's that dark-skinned girl and where does she come from and when is she going home?'

'Of course I didn't!' Connie burst out. 'Now *you're* deciding wrong things about *me*!'

'Whoa.' Abri held up her hand. 'I'm not saying you did, just that you *might* have done, because some people do. Usually not with words but with their eyes. But yours look OK to me.'

Connie was trying to decide if that was a compliment when Thyo rushed back.

'Hey, Abri,' he said, leaning forward on the table. 'There's a man and woman by the escalator having a massive bust-up. You'll get some great pics.'

'Thanks.' Abri rose from her chair and floated off across the hall.

Thyo sat down opposite Connie. 'That got rid of her.'

She glared at him. 'How *dare* you send that email without—'

'Look.' Thyo pushed his phone across the table. It was a good job Connie read quickly, because she forgot to breathe until the end.

From: <research@mexmansol.co.uk>
To Thyomiles@gmail.com

Dear Connie,

I'm over the moon to hear from you! Actually over Jupiter, which is much further away. I can't tell you what it means to get your email after all this time. When you didn't answer my letter last year, I thought that was it. I didn't dare hope – but now I know it's true! – that it was because Mags hadn't passed it on. I don't blame her, of course. How could she know that, ever since I recovered from my illness, you've been the most important thing in

```
my life … even though you haven't been
in my life?

With love - you have no idea how much -
and hoping, hoping, hoping for a reply,

Ben (your dad) X

P.S. Who is Thyo? Please thank him for
letting you use his email.
```

Now Connie remembered to take a huge breath. 'Wow.' She read it again. Then she slid the phone across the table.

Thyo beamed. 'He sounds nice. And excited. And Jupiter is ...' he tapped the phone, 'about seven hundred and fifteen million kilometres away.'

Connie laughed. She found herself leaning across the table and hugging Thyo.

'Lovely.' Abri was standing there again, clicking away. 'I couldn't find the arguing couple. But this'll do nicely.'

Thyo rolled his eyes but didn't look too annoyed. And Connie's heart was too busy doing cartwheels for her to feel awkward.

'Dad told me to get you,' said Abri. 'He's too scared to come over.' Connie looked across the café. Ned was eyeing Hue's box nervously. 'Ma needs collecting from her meeting. Come on, Thyo.' Abri turned and headed over to Ned's table.

'Quick,' Thyo whispered to Connie, 'you need to write back. What do you want to say?' He brandished his phone.

Connie's brain was a snow globe. 'I ... I don't know.' Her whirling thoughts needed to settle before she could possibly decide what – or even *whether* – to reply. 'I need to think.'

Thyo snorted. 'Thinking can be overrated. But suit yourself.' He stood up. 'I guess I'll see you tomorrow then.' He reached over and took a packet of sugar from a pot on the table.

'What's that for?' said Connie.

'Oh.' He looked the closest she'd seen him to being embarrassed. 'I just like to collect something every day.'

'Why?'

'As a souvenir. For a kind of a diary, of objects. They remind me of where I've been, what I've done.'

'Why do you need reminding?'

'I dunno.' He shrugged. 'Maybe because we travel so much. You know that in French the word *souvenir* means memory? Well, my memories are important. They're part of me. If I forget something, it's like a piece of me disappears. Does that sound stupid?'

Connie shook her head, unable to answer. How much had *she* forgotten? How much of *her* had disappeared?

Thyo reached into his pocket and brought out the twig he'd taken from Hue's branch yesterday. 'The day I met my first chameleon.' He grinned. 'And my first Connie.' He waved the sugar packet. 'And this will remind me of the look on your face when you read your dad's email, and of Abri taking photos, and of my dad being scared to come over, and of him tapping his watch over there, and ... gotta go, see you tomorrow. Bye!'

13. Fool's Gold

'I'll have one too,' said Mags.

Connie took two King Cones from the freezer. *She must be really down.* Mags usually ran – OK, walked – a mile from ice creams. 'Trying to lose these,' she'd say, patting her thighs. But now she'd stopped at the newsagent on the way home. And she'd just chosen a chocolate-caramel-creamy-swirly explosion of calories.

'Joe ignored me all morning,' she said. 'And when I gave him that lettuce I picked for Mr Spickles, he didn't even look at me. Just said, "Thanks," and turned to talk to Sue.'

She paid at the counter. 'Let's go and eat these in the park.'

Marching out of the shop, she muttered, 'That woman. Fluttering her false lashes and laughing like a lollipop at everything he says.' Mags looked so upset that Connie didn't mention she'd never heard a lollipop laugh. They walked through the park gate. 'She's all yes Joe, no Joe, tickle my toe, Joe. She's been buttering him up ever since he started at the airport. But what's made him butter me *down*?'

They came to a bench. Mags flopped down and pulled the plastic top off her King Cone. 'I mean, he was grand until yesterday. Did something happen when you were cleaning his room?'

Connie shook her head and said, a bit too quickly, 'Give me that. I'll find a bin.' She took the plastic from Mags. 'Can I do the loop?' It took about forty minutes to walk round the park, and they usually did it together.

But Mags seemed in no mood to move. 'Stay on the path,' she mumbled into her ice cream.

Connie dumped the litter in a bin and headed off. A pigeon hopped beside her. Dogs walked their people. She came to a huge horse chestnut tree. Clamping her ice cream between her teeth, she raised her arms and grabbed the lowest branch. She climbed up between dense leaves that stroked her like giant hands. With every step she felt lighter, freer, as if a cloak were slipping off her shoulders. She sat on a high, hidden branch. Gazing down on passers-by, she saw parts they never would: the bald patch on a man's crown; a woman's grey roots at the back of her head. Such secret knowledge made her feel powerful, calm. She ate her ice cream, scrunching up the wrapper and putting it in her pocket. Then she took out her notebook and scribbled a reply to her dad.

— · —

'Write this,' said Connie the next morning. Across the café table Thyo held his phone with his thumbs at the ready. 'Dear Dad,' she read from her notebook. She stopped. 'No. Dear Mr Fuller. No. Dear – oh dear.' She chewed her cheek. 'What do I call him?'

Thyo looked up. 'How about Ben? Dear Ben. That sounds friendly but not too familiar.'

Connie nodded. 'Dear Ben. No. Dear *Mr* Ben.'

Thyo wrinkled his nose.

'He's *my* dad.' Connie sniffed. 'Dear Mr Ben, thank you for your email. Sorry I've taken so long to answer your letter. You asked about Thyo. His full name is Ichthyosaurus because his mum's a fossil hunter.'

It was Thyo's turn to sniff. 'She's more than that. She studies them and has degrees in them and lectures on them, and now she's going on TV about them. I'll write *palaeontologist* instead.'

'Fine.' Connie shrugged. 'If you can spell it.' She ignored the face he made. 'How *was* her meeting with the film director, by the way?'

'Good and bad. The film's going ahead. But ...' Thyo tilted his head towards the family table. Abri was painting her nails. His parents were talking, not, it seemed, happily. His mum held her palms up in a pleading, persuading kind of way. His dad had a face like a crumpled hanky. 'Ma got this idea that they could hire Dad to draw an artist's impression of the dinosaur. The film crew would use that to make a life-size model and bring it to life with CGI. They'd have scenes of the dinosaur roaming around, two hundred million years ago, between interviews with Ma about digging it up.'

'Sounds brilliant.'

'The director thought so too. But Dad said no, even when they offered him loads of money.'

'Why?'

'You saw how he reacted to your little lizard. He says he'd die of terror if he had to dream up a big one.'

Connie felt sorry for Ned. She might not share his particular fear but ... ever since that terrible day when airport staff had worried and whispered around her, then called the gardaí and social workers, who'd worried and whispered some more before taking her to an emergency foster family, who'd worried and whispered for six whole months while Mags came to visit until she was finally approved as a foster parent ... well, ever since then, Connie had been scared of crowds. Ned had his fear and she had hers but what, really, was the difference? Fear was fear, never mind the cause. 'Poor him,' she murmured.

Thyo snorted. 'Poor *us*, you mean. He hasn't sold a painting for ages and they offered him so much money. Anyway.' He picked up his phone. 'Back to *your* dad.'

Connie read on from her notebook. 'My best friend at school is Ciara Harris.'

She paused again. The next bit said that her best friend at home was Hue. But somehow, she realised, she wasn't ready to share Hue with the man who'd abandoned them both.

She skipped to the next part. 'You asked about my hobbies. Well, I love climbing. I'm going to be the first person up the highest unclimbed mountain – at least, the highest one you're *allowed* to climb. It's in Pakistan and it's called Muchu Chhish.'

Thyo stopped. 'How d'you spell *that*?'

It felt good to be teaching *him* for a change. Connie could spell it backwards; she'd spent long enough gazing at the poster on her bedroom wall. She read out the letters, then went on. 'My favourite biscuits are—'

'Shh!' Thyo hissed. His mum was heading their way.

'Chocolate Hobnobs,' she whispered. 'Love from – no, best wishes from – Connie. Quick, send it.'

Just in time.

'Hi, Connie.' Naledi sat down at their table. 'How are you?'

'Grand,' Connie said shyly in the spotlight of her smile. 'I like your earrings.' Golden discs dangled from Naledi's ears, like flattened snail shells. They gleamed as she moved her head.

'Ammonites.' She fingered an earring. 'They're fossilised sea snails from the Early Jurassic period. I found them on a beach in England. Ned made them into earrings for me. They're iron pyrite: fool's gold. Eh.' She shook her head at Thyo. 'Talking of Ned and fools, your dad won't budge. So I came to cheer myself up with a look at this guy.' She pointed to Hue's box. 'Is that OK, Connie?'

'Sure.' Connie slid the box across the table and on to her lap, out of sight of the café counter.

'I'll go and wash,' said Thyo. 'You got toothpaste, Ma?' Naledi handed him a tube.

When he'd gone, Connie unclipped the lid of Hue's box. Naledi sat still and smiling, gazing at the foliage. At last a blue–purple head poked out between the leaves.

'Ah,' she murmured, 'he's so beautiful.'

Connie could swear Hue understood, the way he slid out, displaying deep blue and green stripes on his back.

'Look at that prehensile tail.'

'Pre– what?' Connie frowned.

'It means his tail can grasp things. It's like an extra leg.' Naledi pointed to the end that coiled tightly round a stem. 'Unusual in reptiles.' She leaned forward. 'Hello there.'

Hue's eyes swivelled upwards, around and back to rest on her, as if pleased with what they saw. 'What's his name?'

'Hue,' said Connie.

Naledi laughed. 'So happy to meet you, Hue.'

Thyo came running back.

'Yoh, that was quick.' Naledi's eyebrows rose. 'Did you clean all those nooks and crannies?'

'Ma,' Thyo groaned. 'You've seen Hue. Bye.'

'I get the message.' Naledi smiled. 'Thanks, Connie.' She stood up and returned to Ned's table.

Thyo whisked out his phone. 'Your dad's written back.'

14. The Emails

From <research@mexmansol.co.uk>

To Thyomiles@gmail.com

Dear Connie,

You're very brave. I'm sure you'll make history as the first person to climb Muchu Chhish.

My turn. Hobbies - well, to be honest, work takes up most of my time. And most of my friends are work colleagues.

I can't believe that Chocolate Hobnobs are your favourite biscuits. Mine too! I think I know your favourite drink, or at least what it used to be. Hot chocolate?

He remembered! Connie felt a catch in her throat.

> Mine is espresso coffee in those tiny
> cups with one teaspoon of sugar. Boring,
> I know, but hey, I'm an adult.
>
> Thyo sounds like an interesting friend.
> Write back soon.
>
> Your ever-loving dad,
>
> Ben

She read it again. Then, 'Write this,' she told Thyo. 'Dear.' She took a deep breath. 'Ben.' Then, she dictated slowly, 'What *is* your work? I looked at the Mexel Mann website but I don't understand it. I've got lots of other questions too. About you, who I remember a bit. And my mum who I don't remember at all. And especially about why you left me.'

Thyo looked up. 'That's a bit ... direct. Are you sure?

Connie nodded quickly and finished dictating. 'Can you send me a photo? Thanks. From Connie.'

Thyo pressed Send and put the phone on the table. An endless minute passed.

Connie made fists in her lap. 'Did I frighten him off?'

'Give him a chance.' But even Thyo looked nervous.

Another minute. 'You were right. I shouldn't have asked.' Connie dug her fingernails into her palms.

Another thirty seconds. 'Maybe he's gone to the toilet,' said Thyo.

Forty seconds more. A stone turned in Connie's stomach.

'Or maybe he's on the phone.'

Another silent minute. Connie put her elbows on the table.

And another. Thyo reached over and squeezed her arm. 'Perhaps he had to go to a meeting. Or maybe—'

The phone buzzed. Connie snatched it.

```
Dear Connie,

Of course I'll answer all your ques-
tions. But not by email. I couldn't
possibly write down everything I have
to say. Which is why I've just done a
crazy thing. I've booked a flight to
Dublin.
```

Connie gasped.

For tomorrow.

She squeaked.

I'll arrive on Ryanair, flight FR503, Terminal 1, at 11.05 am.

She squeaped (gasped *and* squeaked).

If you want to meet me – a very big if, I know – we could go somewhere and talk. For a few hours, or one hour, or fifteen minutes: however long you want. My flight back to Leeds is tomorrow evening.

If you don't want to meet me, I completely understand. I'll come through Arrivals and look around for you. If I don't see you, I'll spend a few hours in Dublin, no problem.

So there's no pressure at all. You don't even have to answer this email. Then you can leave it to the very last minute to choose. And – just a thought, seeing how Mags hid my letter last year – whatever you decide, maybe don't mention anything to her, just for now? We don't want to upset her or make more of this than it is. Why don't we take one step at a time?

Your ever-loving dad, Ben.

P.S. My photo so you'll recognise me (if you want to).

It was small and a bit fuzzy. At first glance he looked like a stranger. But then Connie felt a shock like a match igniting inside her, slow at first, then bursting into flame. She thought she'd forgotten his face. But this photo brought it back: those thick-rimmed glasses and thin cheeks; the dark hair that eight years had sprinkled with grey and chased up his forehead, and a chin that proved chins could be kind.

'Oh,' was all she could say. And a few seconds later, 'Oh.'

She stared at his eyes – *brown like mine!* – with crinkles at the edges. There were crinkles round his mouth too; he must be used to smiling. Her heart was breakdancing as she handed the phone back to Thyo.

'Wow.' He came round the table and sat beside her. Together they read the email again.

'Do you want to meet him?' he said.

'Of course,' she said quickly. And she meant it. She really did. Almost definitely. Probably.

Mags appeared across the hall, wheeling a cleaning trolley.

Connie felt a swirl of dismay and relief. 'But I can't. Like my dad says, Mags would have a fit if she knew.'

Thyo leaned his elbows on the table and rested his chin on his hands. His eyes were wide in his honest, open face. 'So like he *also* says, don't tell her.'

Connie stared at him. Not so honest. Not so open.

'OK,' he said, as if reading her thoughts, 'you'd be going behind her back. But look how long she's gone behind yours.'

Mags opened a door in the wall and pushed the trolley inside.

'You mean meet him here, in secret?' Connie murmured. 'How? She might see us.'

Mags came out of the room without the trolley. She turned to lock the door.

Thyo pressed his lips together. 'Mmm. Where does she clean?'

'The Departures area. That's the floor above this one. But she could still come down at any time. It's too risky.'

'So we have to stop her.' He turned up his palms, as if that would be the easiest thing in the world to do. 'Look, why don't you come to us for lunch and we can work out a plan to—'

Connie shook her head as Mags bustled up.

'Hi, love,' she said. 'I'm all done. Oh.' She looked at Thyo. 'Hello, can I help you?'

He grinned. 'Hi. I'm Thyo. Connie and I met a few days ago.'

'Really?' Mags smiled uncertainly. 'You didn't tell me, Con.'

'Why should I?'

There was an awkward pause. Then Thyo nodded towards the Mileses' table. 'That's my family.' Naledi was hidden behind a newspaper. Ned doodled gloomily on a napkin. Abri was redoing her eyeliner using a steel teapot as a mirror. 'We've been coming here the last few days to—'

'Let his sister take photos,' Connie said, kicking him under the table. 'For her portfolio.' That sounded more impressive than 'use the loos', which Mags would probably disapprove of.

'How nice. Well, good to meet you, Thyo. OK, Con, time to go.'

'Actually.' Thyo stood up. 'We've invited Connie to lunch.'

Mags made a snorty sound, like the horse in the field by Ciara's house that ate grass from Connie's hand. 'Lunch? Well, thank you,' she said stiffly, 'but I'm afraid not. I don't know you.'

Connie winced at her rudeness. 'But I do,' she said, as calmly as she could. If she wanted to persuade Mags – and she *had* to persuade Mags – getting cross wouldn't help.

Thyo's smile didn't crack. 'Come and talk to my ma,' he said breezily. 'Then you'll see it's fine.'

Connie felt like hugging him.

Mags glanced across. Naledi had spread the paper on the table. 'Another time,' she said. 'Let's go, Connie.'

'No,' she blurted. 'I mean, guess what. Thyo's mum is a TV star.'

Mags frowned.

'And a fossil hunter. She's world-famous. They asked her to come to Ireland specially, to make a film about her digging up a dinosaur.'

Mags stared across at Naledi. Even the way she bent over the paper was glamorous. 'Well, maybe I'll just say hello.'

Ned looked up as they approached. Seeing Hue's box in Connie's hand, he jerked back in his chair.

And that was when an idea barged into Connie's brain without knocking. She could help Ned overcome his fear of reptiles *and* persuade Mags to let her visit Thyo's mobile home.

15. Think of the Art

It could have gone worse. But not much.

Connie sat in the back of the Mileses' battered Land Rover between Thyo and Abri. She told herself to be grateful she was there, rather than embarrassed by Mags's behaviour.

It had started well, when Connie suggested her idea. 'Hue could help with Mr Miles's – Ned's – herpetophobia.' It still felt strange using his first name. 'If he gets used to a small reptile first, maybe he'll be OK drawing a big one.'

'Brilliant!' Naledi had clapped her hands.

But Ned had leaned back further in his chair. 'I really don't think that would work.'

'It's a tried-and-tested method,' said Naledi. 'Exposure therapy. Someone who's scared of the dark turns off the light for ten seconds, then twenty, and so on. Someone who's scared of spiders sits closer and closer to a jar with a spider inside, until they can hold it in their hand.'

Ned shuddered.

'Think of the art, Dad,' said Thyo.

'The money,' said Abri.

Ned rubbed his forehead, as if thinking of those things made it sore.

'Isn't it worth a try?' Naledi put her arm round him. 'If it gets too much, you can stop it.'

'Mmf,' he mumbled. From Naledi's wink, Connie guessed that wasn't entirely a no.

Mags cleared her throat. 'Connie tells me you're here for a film shoot. I hope you find our little country agreeable.'

Agreeable? What kind of show-offy word was that? Connie rolled her eyes at Mags's effort to impress the 'TV star'.

But Naledi beamed. 'Oh, more than agreeable. We love it here, don't we, Ned?'

He was staring at Hue's travel box, which Connie carried by her side like a suitcase. 'Is the lid on properly?' He ran his tongue over his top lip.

Naledi tutted. 'What he means is, yes, we love Ireland.'

'I'm so pleased.' Mags tilted her head in what she seemed to think was a dignified way. 'Where are you actually from?'

It was the 'actually' that made Connie's stomach shrink. An 'actually' that made Mags sound like one of those 'What-are-you-doing-here?' people that Thyo had talked about when they'd first met. Even if Mags hadn't meant to offend – and her oblivious smile suggested that she hadn't – would Naledi feel insulted?

Phew. Relief flooded Connie as Naledi chuckled. She was the one who'd taught Thyo to dodge cowpats, after all. 'Oh, a bit of here and a bit of there. Like all of us, when you think about it, hey?'

Now, sitting in the Land Rover, Connie cringed at the memory of Mags's nod: clumsy and clunky and anything but dignified.

Ned had offered to drive but Abri pointed out that he might not be safe with a lizard in the car. Naledi stopped at a garage to buy sandwiches, then turned left off the main road. She smiled in the rear-view mirror. 'How's Hue doing back there?'

'He's grand,' said Connie.

'Good. I'm driving carefully. I know he's a sensitive guy.'

If 'carefully' was this – racing down the road, lurching round corners and scraping the hedges – Connie wondered what normal was like. And never mind Hue, Naledi didn't seem at all worried about her sensitive husband. Ned was leaning forward, as far from the travel box as he could, gripping the sides of the passenger seat.

Ten minutes later they turned through a gate into a field. Connie counted eight mobile homes around the low building of the wash block. Only one home looked occupied. They parked beside its clutter of welly boots, buckets and deckchairs. On the far side of the field, beyond a fence, stretched a band of glittering sea. The blue sky bubbled with clouds.

Ned opened the car door and rushed to the mobile home. Unlocking the door, he disappeared inside.

'Ah, Ned.' Naledi sighed. 'Come on, Connie, let's bring Hue in.'

It was like a house that had shrunk in the wash. On the left was a little kitchen area with a cooker, a fridge and cupboards on the wall. Connie felt a rush of sharp heat, like Lemsip flooding her chest, to think of this roving family, free to travel anywhere. She was the opposite: nailed to the ground for eight years and thinking – until now – that she had no real family at all. 'It's lovely,' she murmured.

Coming in behind her, Abri snorted. 'Wait till you need the toilet.' She pointed out of the window at a tall narrow tent to the left of the mobile home. 'We have to use that until the water's fixed. We're the only idiots staying here.'

On the right was a table with benches either side. Beyond the table was a closed door. And beyond *that*, Connie guessed, were the bedrooms, where Ned must have fled.

'Put the box on the table,' said Naledi. 'We'll give Hue a chance to settle.'

Connie and Thyo sat on the benches while Abri went through the door to the bedrooms.

'Is that your diary?' Connie pointed to the opposite wall.

The July page of a calendar had been torn out and taped to the wall. Objects were sellotaped to each square. The first of July had a pebble and 2 July a tiny shell. The twig from Hue's box was stuck across 3 July and on 4 July was the sugar packet from yesterday.

Thyo took a scrap of paper from his pocket and some Sellotape from the table. 'I wrote it down,' he said, taping the scrap to 5 July, today, 'so I'll spell it properly when I send you a congratulations card for climbing it.'

Mucho Chhish

Connie grinned. She peered through the slits of Hue's box. She nodded at Naledi. 'His back is blue and green, so he's pretty relaxed.'

Naledi went to the door beyond the table and knocked. 'Ned,' she called, 'you can come out.' She waited a few seconds. 'Ned?' Shaking her head, she went through the door.

Thyo sat down again beside Connie. Naledi returned with Ned in tow. Abri followed, freshly lipsticked in purple. She pushed past Ned in the doorway. His face was the colour of raw pastry.

'I'm sure Hue's as scared as you are,' Connie said.

Clutching the door handle, he managed a little smile.

'Here.' Naledi sat at the table and patted the chair beside her. 'Just sit for a bit, get used to looking at the box.'

Ned didn't move.

Abri pointed to the table. 'Dad,' she said sternly. 'That is a plastic box. Inside the box is a frightened little creature with a tiny brain. You could step on him. He can't possibly get out unless you lift the lid. He isn't poisonous. He doesn't sting. He doesn't bite.'

'Well actually—' began Connie. Thyo jabbed her with his elbow. Now wasn't the time to say that Hue's bite could be pretty sore.

'Think of the money,' said Abri.

'The art,' said Thyo.

'All yours,' said Naledi.

Ned edged towards the table. Everyone clapped as he sat down. His hand crept towards the box, then shot back and dropped into his lap.

'Art,' said Thyo.

'Money,' said Abri.

'Yours,' said Naledi.

He raised his hand again, reached out and – yes! He tapped the box with his fingertip, then pulled it back quickly. Thyo whooped and everyone else clapped.

'Shh,' Connie put a finger to her lips. It was all very well cheering Ned on, but what about poor Hue inside?

After four minutes Ned could rest a fingertip on the box for ten seconds. After two more, it lasted twenty seconds. And three minutes later, four fingertips touched the box for thirty seconds.

'It's gonna be a long afternoon,' Thyo muttered.

'We need to plan for tomorrow,' Connie whispered.

Thyo turned to his mum. 'Can Connie and I take our lunch to the beach?'

'Well,' Naledi looked at Ned, who'd withdrawn his hand and was rubbing his fingertips. 'Someone should stay here with Dad. I have to go to the site. I said I'd cover for the team while they go to lunch.'

'I'll stay.' Abri sat at the table. She brought out her phone. 'Why don't I take some photos of Hue, Dad? Looking at them might help you get used to him.'

And that's when Connie's second brainwave came knocking.

16. A Skull and a Claw

Half an hour later, Connie explained her idea to Thyo. They were sitting on a rock, eating lunch and dangling their feet in the sea. Naledi had walked with them a little way, but now she was safely out of earshot, heading towards the fossil site further along the beach.

'That *could* work.' Thyo took a bite of his sandwich. 'Though it means you'll have to tell Abri about your dad.'

'No it doesn't,' said Connie. 'I'll keep it vague, say it's for her portfolio. I'll tell Mags that too.' She tore off a corner of her sandwich and threw it to a seagull that was eyeing them greedily from the next rock.

'So we've definitely decided to meet your dad, then? Yay!' He raised his hand for a high five.

She loved the way he said 'we'. They'd only met two days ago and already he was sharing her adventure.

If only she shared his confidence in return. 'No,' she said. 'I mean, I'm still not sure.'

'Why not?' Thyo dropped his hand. 'If you don't like him, you never have to see him again. What have you got to lose?'

Connie hugged her knees and stared out to sea. 'My dreams,' she said softly. 'What if he's awful?'

Thyo opened his mouth. Then closed it. Not even he had an answer for that.

They finished their sandwiches in silence.

'Guys!'

Connie turned. Further down the pebbly beach, Naledi stood at the bottom of a cliff. She was waving madly. 'Over here – you've got to see this!'

'Come on,' said Thyo, looking relieved at the distraction. They pulled on their socks and shoes and raced along the beach. Connie's wet feet slipped inside her trainers but she still outran Thyo to the cliff.

A patch of the rock face had been fenced off. There was a gate in the fence with a sign that said 'University staff only'. Naledi had undone the padlock and was inside, crouching at the foot of the cliff with her rucksack beside her. She picked at the rock with a tool like a screwdriver.

Connie stopped at the fence to catch her breath. She gazed up at the cliff. It was made of slanting layers of dark and lighter rock.

Naledi stood up as Thyo arrived. She was smiling from dangly earring to dangly earring.

'Look,' she said, pointing at the cliff. 'Can you see how the rock is layered? The dark layers are hard, and the layers in between are softer. And the hard layers stick out a bit because the softer layers have been more worn down by wind and water.'

Connie came through the gate in the fence and stood at the cliff face. She ran her fingers over a hard, smooth layer. What a journey these rocks had taken; what secrets they must hold.

'And here,' said Naledi, crouching again, 'is our treasure.'

She touched a lump, about twenty centimetres long, which bulged up from a hard layer into the softer layer above it.

Connie hunkered down beside her.

'Oh,' she said. A lump like this in a rock wasn't what she imagined when she thought of dinosaur remains. She'd expected a skeleton, or at least a pile of bones.

Naledi laughed. 'It might not look much, Connie, but it's a skull. We're clearing all round it before we dig it out.'

Connie screwed up her eyes. 'A dinosaur skull?'

'We think so, yes,' said Naledi. With the tip of her screwdriver tool, she traced two curving lines of darker fragments in the lump. They looked a bit like an open zip. 'That's the mouth. And those notches are the teeth. Blunt for grinding plants, so we know it was a herbivore.'

'Like Stegosaurus?' Connie remembered the collection of little plastic dinosaurs Mags had given her on her sixth birthday. They'd learned all the names together, and Connie had told Hue that these were his great-great-great-great-etcetera-grandparents.

'A lot older than Steg,' said Naledi. 'We think these rocks were laid down around two hundred million years ago.'

Connie couldn't imagine that many millions. Mags was forty-six and that was old enough.

Naledi pointed to a circle above the zip-mouth. 'This is the eye socket. And look what I've just noticed.' She moved the tip of the tool to the edge of the socket. 'This is *really* something.' She traced a faint triangle, slightly darker than the surrounding rock. It pointed from the edge of the eye socket into the forehead of the skull, just below where the eyebrows would be.

If dinosaurs had eyebrows. Connie grinned at the thought.

'I'd say it's either a tooth or a claw,' said Naledi, 'and it's embedded in the eye socket.'

'Wow!' said Thyo, who'd crouched down beside Connie to look. 'You mean from another dinosaur?'

His mother nodded. 'Probably a claw. A tooth would be longer and thinner. And it's more likely that a predator would claw at an eye than bite it. My guess is that a big carnivore attacked our herbivore here, and one of its claws broke off in the fight. The poor herbivore lost its life. The carnivore just lost a fingernail and got away.'

'A carnivore ... like a T-rex, maybe?' Thyo's eyes went wide.

Naledi laughed. 'I know you'd love that, but I don't think so. What we have here is older than T-rex. It could be a Megalosaurus. A Meg bone has been found in Ireland before.'

Megalosaurus. The word thundered round Connie's head. To think that a mighty meat-eater could have lived in little Ireland, or whatever Ireland was back then.

'What about our poor old herbivore?' she said, nodding at the lump of fossil skull.

'We don't know yet. If we could find something else – another bone or two – it might help us to identify it.' Naledi shielded her eyes with a hand and peered up at the rock face. 'See how this layer runs up the cliff? There could be more fossils up there. We'll need scaffolding to get up and have a proper—'

'Connie!' yelled Thyo.

But she was already climbing the cliff. The harder rock layers jutted out, giving something for her fingers to grip and her feet to stand on. She scrambled up the nearly vertical cliff face lightly and quickly.

'Come *down!*' cried Naledi. 'It's not safe!'

She was right. Connie's left foot slipped, sending down a cloud of stones.

Don't look down, she told herself.

Her foot scrabbled against the cliff, dislodging more crumbly rock. At last it found a tiny step that held. She climbed faster until she was almost running up the rock face. Every muscle, nerve and thought focused on the next foothold, the next ledge, a cranny here, a jutting root there, a burst of tiny purple flowers and ...

Connie hauled herself over the top of the cliff and lay panting on the heather. When her heart had dropped back into her chest, she swivelled round on her stomach, stuck her head over the edge of the cliff and waved.

17. More Fossils and a Photo

'You made it!' Thyo shouted. Connie leaned out further from the edge and did a thumbs-up.

Beside him, Naledi roared, 'Get back from the edge!'

Connie ignored her, looking down the cliff face. There was a wind up here, bullying clouds across the sky. The sun flashed, then dimmed, now lighting up the cliff, now plunging its nooks and crannies into shadow.

'I said, get back! Those rocks are crumbly.'

'Hey!' Connie yelled. 'I can see something.'

She was looking down into a crevice in the cliff, between two layers of rock. The upper, softer layer had worn away. She could see dark fragments in the top surface of the harder rock. They were arranged like pieces of a mosaic inside a rough circle.

'You can only see it from above,' she called down.

'For the last time, get back!' But the panic in Naledi's voice was now spiced with excitement.

And that was enough for Connie. She spun round on her stomach and dropped her legs down the cliff. Ignoring the cries from below, she climbed down until her face was level with the crevice. She slipped her hand inside and felt the surface.

'They're darker bits of rock,' she shouted. 'Curved. And bumpy. Knobbly, like the skin of an orange.'

'OK. Now get down here!'

At last Connie obliged, dancing down the rock face so fast it felt as if she barely touched it.

'You're mad,' Thyo gasped, though his eyes shone with awe, as she landed on the beach.

Naledi clasped a hand to her chest. 'Oh, thank goodness.' She shook her head. 'What if you'd—?'

'I didn't,' said Connie brightly, brushing rock dust off her front. 'And you seemed to think it was worth looking at.'

Now that Connie was safe, Naledi's excitement took over. 'Sure was.' She took a pair of binoculars from her rucksack and stared up the cliff, tweaking and twisting, letting out little squeaks of frustration. 'Ah, I can't see properly. We need to get that scaffolding up.'

— · —

'You actually *climbed* that?'

'Without a rope?'

'Unbelievable!'

The praise came thick and fast when the dig team returned from lunch. The four men looked to Connie like one big beard divided into people. They were so loud and keen that her tongue turned to fudge when they asked her to describe what she'd found.

As the men set up the scaffolding, Connie and Thyo returned to the campsite. They climbed the fence into the field and headed across to the mobile home.

'Hang on.' Thyo stopped outside and pointed through the window. Ned was sitting at the table with his back to them. Abri sat opposite, holding up her phone.

She saw Thyo and put a finger to her lips.

Because there, in the middle of the table, was Hue, all blue, green and red contentment. Ned's arm was on the table, his fingers spread like a starfish. Hue raised a front leg. It hovered over Ned's hand for a few seconds. Then Ned jerked his arm back.

Connie and Thyo bumped fists and went inside.

'Well done, Dad,' said Thyo.

Abri showed them her phone. There was a photo of a small, red, two-pronged foot above a large, pale, five-pronged hand. 'Great for my portfolio,' she said. 'Imagine the stories you could make up about that picture.'

Connie couldn't have scripted it better. It led perfectly to her plan for Operation Distract-Mags-Tomorrow. 'Actually,' she said, glancing at Thyo, 'I had another idea for your portfolio. You know how you're photographing passengers waiting at the airport? What about the people who are there every day?'

— · —

'Me?' said Mags, that evening at dinner. 'Why would Abri want to photograph me?'

'Because she says it's sad how some people don't even notice the cleaners,' said Connie. 'She wants to show what a great job you do.'

'Well, how nice!' Mags ran a hand over her hair. 'Wish I'd known earlier. I'd have had a trim.'

'Where will you be cleaning tomorrow?' Connie said, as lightly as she could over her thundering heart.

'I'm in Terminal 1 Departures all week. I can come down and fetch Abri on my break at eleven.'

'No!' Connie burst out, anything but lightly. Dad's plane was due to land at five past eleven; what if it arrived early? 'I mean,' she added, organising a smile, 'it makes more sense for Abri to come up and meet you in the cleaners' break room. It'll save you a trip.'

'I s'pose so. Grand.'

'Lovely chicken, by the way,' Connie said quickly. 'Can I have some more?'

18. Arrival

Connie's stupidphone said it was ten twenty-three AM. So where was Thyo? And, more importantly, where was Abri? Of all the days to be late! The Arrivals screen said the plane was on time. That meant her dad would land in forty-one minutes and – she looked at her phone again – thirty-two seconds. But Thyo was normally here by ten o'clock. And now there were only – another glance – forty-one minutes and twenty-nine seconds until ...

Stop it, she told herself. She couldn't sit here phone-watching for the next ... her eyes found the screen again. *Stop it!*

She distracted herself by studying the arriving passengers as they came through the sliding doors. A young man wearing long flowery shorts. A very tall lady with a very small man. An exhausted-looking mother and father, each with a child on their shoulders, another child riding each of their trolleys and another one hanging off each of their arms. A cool-looking man in a cool-looking jacket, so busy on his cool-looking phone that he bumped into a pillar, which wasn't cool at all.

Where were they coming from, where were they going, all these stories on legs, full of histories and hopes, secrets and dreams? Take that man with a guitar case slung over his shoulder. Was there really an instrument inside or was the case stuffed with diamonds? Or elephant tusks? Or cheeses, or mini-pugs? Or—

'Sorry we're late.' And there was Thyo, almost crashing into the table. He pulled out a chair and sat down. 'We had to go to the site first because the scaffolding's up and Ma wanted to look at your fossil.'

My fossil. Despite her flittering nerves, Connie felt a surge of pride.

'Or rather *fossils.* Because guess what?' Thyo gabbled. 'She thinks you found dinosaur eggs! The curved pieces of rock are broken bits of eggshell and they're inside a kind of circle because it was a nest. So she's come up with this story that maybe the mother was defending the nest when the predator came and clawed through her eye socket, which would be amazing evidence that dinosaurs protected their young, which is apparently big news in the dinosaur world, and I said that's great, Ma, now can we go to the airport, and she said since when was I so keen to wash, and it was hard to hurry her up without explaining the real reason, and in the end we left her at the site and—'

'Where's Abri?' Connie could see Thyo's dad standing at the café counter, but there was no sign of his sister.

'Where do you think? Doing her face in the loo.'

'She'd better be quick.'

Ned came over with two scones on plates. 'There you go.' He put them on the table. 'No Hue today? I thought maybe we could, ah ...' He cleared his throat. 'Carry on making friends.'

'He was a bit off-colour this morning,' Connie lied. The real reason she'd left him at home was due to land in – she glanced at her phone – fourteen minutes and thirty-four seconds. She didn't want Hue there to distract them.

'Sorry to hear that,' said Ned, looking almost as if he meant it. 'Well, there's Abri. I'm off to wash.' He walked towards the loo as she came out.

Abri floated up to their table in a pink crop top and spotty blue-and-white trousers that would fail stupendously on anyone else, but on her looked, well, stupendous. 'Hi, Connie. So where do I find Mags?'

'In the cleaners' break room on the fifth floor. I told her you'll need about an hour together.'

'At least,' said Thyo. 'See you here at a quarter past twelve. Earliest.'

Abri curled her lip. 'You trying to get rid of me?'

'Course we are,' said Thyo, blowing her a kiss. 'Bye, sis.'

Connie glared at him. Was he *trying* to give the game away? But his answer seemed to satisfy Abri. She waved and drifted off.

Siblings. They were more confusing than long division.

Connie glanced at her phone. Two minutes past eleven. She went over to the Arrivals screen.

Leeds Flight FR503 landed 10.57

She came back breathless, even though it was only nine steps away. 'It's early. It can't be!'

Thyo jumped up. 'Oh.' He pushed his chair in. 'Right.' He bounced his fists together. 'He'll only have hand luggage.' He bit his thumb. 'So he'll be out soon. You should go to the barrier.'

Connie froze. 'I can't,' she whispered.

'What?' Thyo stared at her.

She looked down, unable to meet his gaze. Her eyes fell on Ned's untouched scones. Of course: there was her excuse.

'What if Dave the café man sees me meeting someone off the plane? He might call Mags.'

'You should've thought of that!' Thyo hissed. 'After all this – you've *got* to go through with it!'

She looked at the Arrivals doors. People were streaming through them. Her feet were lead. She shook her head. And gasped.

Because there he was. The man from the photo, in a grey suit, walking through the Arrivals doors on quick, efficient legs. He stopped at the barrier and looked round the hall.

Connie shrank in her chair. 'Don't catch his eye,' she murmured. 'He mustn't see me.'

But Thyo was already heading towards the barrier. Connie slid from her chair and dived behind a pillar at the edge of the café.

19. The Shortest Half Hour in History

Crouching behind the pillar, Connie couldn't hear the conversation between Thyo and the man – HER DAD! But she could see the man – HER DAD! – nodding, then walking towards the sliding exit doors. He was shorter than she remembered. But that made sense: of course he'd have looked taller to her four-year-old self. He seemed to bounce rather than walk, as if he had springs in his heels. He went through the exit doors.

Three seconds later, Thyo was back by her side. 'If you're trying not to be noticed,' he said, 'you might want to rethink.' At the café counter Dave was frowning across at her, still crouched by the pillar. She wobbled to her feet on legs made of porridge.

'I'll go and distract Dave,' said Thyo. 'Tell him you're feeling faint or something, which is why you're doing frog impressions. I'll say you need some fresh air. Your dad's waiting outside.'

Connie had no idea how she got there. But there she was, standing on the pavement, her mouth slightly open and her voice glued to her throat.

The man-Dad blinked through his glasses. Was it Connie's imagination or did his eyes glimmer with tears? A smile flashed, then fled from his face.

'Hello, Connie.' He held out his hand. 'I'm ... I'm your – I'm Ben.'

In one of their dream-meetings – and there had been many – Connie had fallen into his arms while he'd sobbed and apologised for ever leaving her. In another, she'd stood cold and still, shooting eight years of anger into his miserable little heart. But now she did neither. Reaching out her arm, she grazed rather than shook his hand. Her head roared with unsayable things: *Pleased to meet you ... Not pleased to meet you ... How are you? ... How dare you!* But all her mouth allowed was 'Hi.' Their eyes collided. She dropped hers. They rested on his tie. Another word fell out. 'A chameleon!'

It was sewn on to the dark blue silk, a shimmery shape made of some kind of translucent material. Its back was green and its stomach red.

The man-Dad-Ben gave another smile. And this time it took charge of his face. 'This is Camelia. I wore her just in case you didn't recognise me. I knew a chameleon would mean something to my Connie.'

Your Connie? The words were just sinking in when he put a hand in his back pocket. And never mind the awkwardness: she burst out laughing. The chameleon's back turned from green to orange to yellow. Its stomach flashed purple.

'How does it do that?'

'Wires and a switch,' Mr Ben-Dad said, flipping his tie over to show her. 'Like Christmas lights.'

Connie giggled again.

He looked down the pavement, then through the glass doors into the Arrivals hall. 'No Mags?'

Connie shook her head.

Mr Ben-Dad gave a quick nod. 'Best for now,' he murmured. Connie could sense his relief. 'She's probably no fan of mine.' He rubbed his chin with a fingertip as if to wipe off an imaginary stain. 'Hardly surprising.' He tapped his lip. 'Where shall we go?'

Connie had been so busy planning Mags's distraction, she hadn't thought of that. Across the road was a car park with a few shops beside it. 'Over there?'

Ben-Dad nodded and led the way over the zebra crossing to the shops. He stopped at a kind of café-cum-newsagent. They sat at a plastic table outside. 'Can I get you something?' He pointed through the window to the drinks and sandwiches.

'No, thanks.' Connie's twittery fingers would spill it, or her jittery nerves would puke it up. Plus it would waste their precious time.

Not that she knew how to fill that time. Silence set between them like invisible cement. At last she said, 'How was your flight?' She bit her cheek. After eight years – of all the stupid questions!

'Fine.' And the smile wrapped round the word told Connie that it wasn't stupid: that he understood how she felt. 'Except I was so nervous that I spilled my orange juice over the lady next to me. Who called me a few names you might not want to hear. Or you might.'

Connie gave a little smile back.

'And I was shaking so much that the pilot reported turbulence. Which was great for me because the lady was still calling me names but all I heard was "Fmm" because her false teeth fell out.'

Connie's smile widened.

'Then her wig flew off,' he continued, 'and went whizzing round the plane. Someone yelled there was a flying poodle on board. And a passenger who worked in animal rescue said we had to let it out, so the pilot flew the plane down and landed on the Irish Sea. But when a flight attendant opened the emergency door, well ...' He tutted. 'The wig fell out and sank. Everyone thought the flying poodle had drowned. And the animal rescue guy got into big trouble. Trouble as big as a truck.' He shook his head. 'No, as big as a tractor. No, a tank. No, a tower of ...' He looked at Connie, his eyebrows arching.

'T-rexes?' she said shyly.

'Terrific!' Ben-Dad clapped. 'And you weren't even there.'

As they laughed, a fist unclenched in Connie's chest. He was fun. And his nervousness proved that he really did care.

He reached for her hand across the table, then thought better of it and stopped. 'Thank you,' he said quietly, 'for meeting me. It must be hard.'

Hard? Maths was hard. Cheese could be too. And luck, when something wasn't your fault. But a disappearing dad? Hard wasn't the half of it – or the hundredth. The fist clenched inside her again. 'Why did you leave me?' she burst out.

You'd think she'd shot him, the way he flinched in his chair. 'I was expecting that. But not quite so soon. I was ill, Connie. In the head. It's a long story.' His eyes were doing that glimmery thing again.

'And eight years is a long time.' She hadn't meant to snap, but there were crocodiles in her throat.

'I know.' He put his fingertips to his temples. 'That's why I've come here. To tell you what happened, what led up to that day when I ...' He slipped his fingers under his glasses and rubbed his eyes. 'It's hard to know where to start.'

'How about with my mum?' Again, the crocodiles snatched at her voice.

'She ...' He dropped his eyes.

'I know.' Connie swallowed. 'But how?'

He picked an invisible crumb from the table. 'A car crash.'

Connie put a hand to her mouth.

'A car smashed into ours. I was driving. Hardly hurt.' He closed his eyes. 'On the outside. But your mum was in the passenger seat. And her parents – your grandparents – were in the back. And they all ...' He stopped, shaking his head.

Connie's hand fell to her lap. She took a deep, steadying breath. 'How old was I?'

He opened his eyes slowly, as if the lids had suddenly put on weight. 'Two and a bit. You'd just started at a day nursery. Thank goodness.' He spread his hands on the table and frowned, as if he'd never seen them before. 'Otherwise you'd have been in the car too.'

'What happened after they ... the accident?' Her voice was a whisper.

A muscle bulged in his cheek. 'Over the next year or so, I sort of gave up. I couldn't get up in the mornings. I could hardly wash or make breakfast. I was a ghost of a person. And ghosts make rubbish dads, Connie. I wasn't safe to look after you.'

'Why didn't I go to my other grandparents? Or an aunt or uncle?'

He rubbed his fingers over his face like a moving beard. 'My parents died before you were born. I was an only child, and so was your mum. So it was just you, me and your mum – Lara.'

Lara. The name was full of laughter and danced round Connie's head. 'What was she like?'

'Connie!'

She looked up. For a second her vision was fuzzy. She blinked into focus – and there was Thyo, standing a few respectful metres away. He jabbed his watch and mouthed, 'Time.'

The shortest half hour in history. 'I have to go,' she said, standing up.

Ben-Dad blinked. 'Oh, right. Yes.'

'But I've got loads more questions.'

'Of course you have.' He stood up and pushed his chair in. 'Maybe we could meet later?'

'Not today.'

'Tomorrow? I can find a hotel, stay the night.' He looked as desperate as she felt not to leave it like this.

She nodded. 'Ten-thirty. Here. Bye.'

No handshake, no hug. Just a funny little wave as she rushed off to Thyo, her heart in her throat and her head in a washing machine.

20. Thank You, Egg

They hurried back to the Pie in the Sky café and sat a few tables away from Ned.

He glanced up from his newspaper and waved.

Thyo leaned across the table towards Connie. 'So, how did it go? He seemed nice.'

She gave a quick nod. 'I ... I have to let it all sink in. I'm seeing him again tomorrow. He's going to stay another night.'

Thyo sat upright. 'But what about Mags? How will you distract her again?'

Connie hadn't thought of that. 'Maybe Abri can do another photo shoot?' But that idea died when a scowling Abri returned with Mags a few minutes later.

'She got me cleaning toilets.' Abri flumped down in a chair.

Mags patted her shoulder. 'I knew you'd get better photos if you stepped into my shoes.'

'That's not all I stepped in,' Abri muttered.

— · —

It was a quiet, slow afternoon, at least on the outside. Connie sat in the car while Mags banged on about how good it was for snowflake teens to learn there was more to life than eyeliner. Arriving home, she went up to her room and said hello to Hue, then climbed the North Ridge (1960) to her think pad.

On the inside, though, it was athletic. Connie's stomach did high jumps, her heart hurdled, and a single question sprinted round her head. Sitting on her bed, she leaned down towards the loft opening. 'How will we keep Mags busy tomorrow, Hue?'

He eyed her coldly from his cage. Then, slowly and elegantly, like a ballet dancer in treacle, he turned his back on her. She could swear he was saying, 'We? You left me at home today, so sort it out yourself.'

'He had this amazing chameleon tie,' she said, as if to make amends. But Hue's bottom clearly wasn't impressed because it vanished into the foliage, leaving nothing but his tail sticking out. It struck her that she hadn't even asked Dad why he'd left a chameleon with her all those years ago.

'OK,' she sighed, 'you can come with me tomorrow. But you'd better behave.'

Her eye caught the poster of Muchu Chhish that she'd stuck on the opposite wall. 'How will I distract Mags?' She imagined she was standing on top of the mountain looking down. But none of the glaciers, slopes or valleys spread out below her could help.

After ten minutes she gave up and went downstairs to the kitchen to get some lunch. And, as she opened the fridge, the answer jumped out at her. Or rather it sat there, gazing from a rack in the door, calm and silent.

'Thank you, egg,' she whispered.

She spent the afternoon rehearsing her lines and practising expressions in the mirror. By the time she came down for dinner, everything was clear in her mind except the timing. That would have to wait until tomorrow.

— · —

Connie was carefully late for breakfast next morning. She came into the kitchen with Hue in his travel box.

'Sorry,' she said, yawning loudly. 'I overslept.'

'It's a shame you can't have a lie-in, love. But no choice until Janey's back, I'm afraid.'

'That's OK.' Connie tried not to show how absolutely-OK-and-in-fact-perfect it was. Mags pushed the cornflakes box towards her across the table. 'Actually,' Connie said, as casually as she could, 'I think I'll have a boiled egg.'

'Well, hurry up, then. I'd have put one on for you if I'd known.'

'You go and get ready.' Connie took a saucepan and egg cup from the cupboard. 'I'll be quick.'

She closed the kitchen door behind Mags. Then she turned the saucepan upside down and put it on the draining board, as if it had been used and was drying. She did the same with the egg cup, a teaspoon and a plate.

Mags came downstairs ten minutes later to find Connie waiting in the hall with Hue in his box. The kitchen door was closed. Mags put on her jacket and slung her bag over her shoulder. Connie followed her out, slamming the front door behind her. She sat in the back seat with Hue's box on her lap. As Mags started the car, Connie took out her phone. *Eight twenty-six.*

Three green traffic lights, four red ones and two busy roundabouts later, they arrived at the airport. *Eight forty-eight.* After a walk from the car park they reached the Pie in the Sky café. *Eight fifty-three.* The whole journey, house to café, had taken twenty-seven minutes.

Connie found a table. 'Are you on Departures again?' she said, hoping she sounded casual.

Mags nodded. 'Have a good morning, love. I'll see you at one.'

Connie waved her off up the escalator. She put Hue's box on the table and took her notebook and pen from her jacket. She needed to work out how long she'd have with her dad later, when her plan kicked in and she'd got Mags out of the way. But writing down the numbers, her idea didn't seem quite as brilliant as yesterday.

3 green lights + 4 red lights + 2 busy roundabouts + walk between car park and café
took 27 min.

If all lights are green and no hold-ups, the
shortest travel time is about

She chewed her pen.

22 min each way?
Add 5 min for Mags to go in and out of
house.
That's 44 + 5 = Total 49 min.
Time taken for me to walk across to meet
Dad: 3 min.
And back again afterwards: another 3 min.
Total: 6 min.

So, time I can spend with Dad:
49 min - 6 min = 43 min.
40 min to be safe.

'Dammit, Hue,' she muttered to the box. 'Forty measly minutes to catch up on eight enormous years. Better use it well.'

She was jotting down her most important questions when Thyo's grin appeared, followed swiftly by the rest of him.

'The good news,' he said, pulling out a chair, 'actually the *great* news, is that the director wants you to be in the film.'

'Me?' Connie dropped her pen. 'But I don't know anything about fossils.'

'You don't have to. Ma told him about the nest. And he wants you to re-enact finding it. You'll be famous.'

'I don't want to be famous. Not in that way.' She couldn't think of anything worse than acting in front of thousands, maybe millions, of viewers.

'All you have to do is climb the cliff again. *With* a rope this time, for health and safety, so it'll be easy for you. You don't have to say anything.'

'Really? Wow. Well, can I think about it?'

'You'll have to think fast.' Thyo sat down. 'Because the bad news is that our water's being fixed today so that the film crew can stay on the campsite. Which means we won't need to come here again to wash.'

'Oh.' Connie felt something crumble in her chest, like a sandcastle when the tide comes in. She'd had more excitement in the last week than she'd had for ages, if not for ever, thanks to Thyo. Without his confidence, kindness and – to be honest – cheek, she'd never have met her dad.

'But you have to come over again. Not just for the filming. I mean any time. How do we stay in touch?'

Her stupidphone had its uses. Taking it from her pocket, Connie gave him her number then looked at the time. Ten-nineteen. 'Quick, go back to your table. I have to do something. I'll explain later. If Dave asks where I am, say I've gone to another café for a change.'

She pressed Mags's number.

'Connie? Everything OK?'

'Yes. No. I think I left the gas ring on. When I boiled my egg this morning.'

'What? Are you sure?'

'Yes, I mean, I think so.'

There was a tutting noise. Then a silence of swallowed swear-words. Then, 'For goodness' sake!' The phone went dead as Mags ended the call.

Four agonising minutes later, she appeared. 'I've told Joe – Mr Dooley – I have to go. He's not best pleased. And neither am I.'

When Mags had gone through the exit and turned right towards the staff car park, Connie stood up and took Hue's box from the table. She put her phone in her pocket, glancing at the time. Ten twenty-seven. Perfect.

21. A Painful Past

The minute she saw Ben-Dad, Connie's memorised questions flew from her head. And the polite handshake she'd planned turned into a kind of hug-shake, as her hand met his open arms.

It was OK, though, because he covered her embarrassment with his own question.

'What's that?' He pointed to Hue's box, which she carried in her left hand. 'A travel box? For a ... no! Don't tell me you've still got a chameleon?'

'I've still got *Hue*,' she said proudly. 'And this is the box you left him in, remember?'

'Good grief!' He clapped a hand to his head. 'I knew I recognised it. And that means Hue's more than eight years old! You must have taken fantastic care of him. I have to see this immortal creature.'

'Not here. It's a bit noisy for him.' That was her excuse to move to a more discreet place. 'There's a café in Terminal 2.' This part of the plan was crucial. It was all very well getting rid of Mags, but Terminal 1 was still too risky. If Dave or Mr Dooley-Joe or someone saw them together, Mags would hear of it as soon as she returned.

Five minutes later they were sitting in a café in Terminal 2. Connie put Hue's box on the table. She unclipped the lid.

Ben-Dad peered inside. 'Well hello, little chap.'

Hue's head poked purply out, between leaves. His eyes played pinball, eyeing Ben-Dad on one side, Connie on the other and everything in between.

'Do you think he remembers you?' she said.

Ben-Dad smiled. 'If only he were that smart!'

'It sometimes feels like he is. Like he understands everything.'

'A kind of talking animal?' Ben-Dad laughed. 'That would be fun. But chameleons are very primitive. Their colour changes are all for survival: stuff like temperature control and danger and mating. I suppose you could call it a language, but it's a very basic one.'

'How do you know so much about chameleons?'

'I've studied them for years.' He laid a hand on Hue's box. 'Their brains might be simple but their bodies are amazing. I showed you one when you were tiny and you loved it. So after your mum ...' He pressed his lips together. 'I bought Hue for you as a pet. You took him everywhere – the supermarket, the doctor's, the park – in his box, of course. And out of it, too; you even wanted him around when you had a bath. I'd put out some food by the taps and he'd sit there and eat.'

A vague picture came into Connie's mind. She was sitting in a bath playing with a green boat. In front of her, clinging to a silver tap, was a blue chameleon. Or maybe the boat was blue and the chameleon green; she couldn't remember. Doubt muddied her mind. *Was* she remembering, or just imagining the scene from his description?

'You two were inseparable,' Ben-Dad said, so gently that an unexpected anger burst out of her.

'Unlike us two! Why did you walk away from me?'

He caught his top lip in his teeth. 'I was sick, Connie. I was taking ...' He paused. 'Medication. But there were side effects. I started having strange turns. I'd been off work for months. I thought a holiday would do us good.

A change of scene, somewhere not too far, like Ireland. But when we arrived here, I had another turn, in the café.'

'What do you mean "turn"?'

He shook his head. 'I don't know: a kind of blackout, where I forgot everything around me. I remember sitting at our table, getting up and talking to Mags. I went to the bathroom and took some medicine.' He took a long breath. 'Too much. Because the next thing I remember is waking up in hospital. They told me I'd been in a coma for fourteen months.'

'*Fourteen months?*' Connie pressed a hand to her mouth. 'What sort of medicine does that?'

'A sort that hasn't been tested. I was trying out a new kind.' He frowned down at his hands. 'It's complicated, Connie. I'd have to show you my work to explain. I wish I could, one day.' He adjusted his glasses on his nose. 'Anyway, the doctors thought I'd never wake up. And when I did, they couldn't understand what had happened any more than I could.'

'How *awful,*' she murmured, her anger evaporating.

He nodded. 'Especially when I asked about you. They said you were fine and safe, but I couldn't see you until they'd run tests on my brain function. I was in and out of consciousness for another three months. Whenever I asked for you, they kept saying things like "Soon," and "You need to get well first, Mr Fuller." And I didn't get well for a long time. I kept having blackouts, and going back and forth to hospital, and feeling sad and hopeless. The courts ruled I was unfit to look after you, even to see you.'

'How could they?' Connie's throat was full of dust.

'They said it was in your best interest. That you were safe and happy with Mags and it could upset you too much to see me. And no doubt Mags agreed.'

No doubt. Fury tore through Connie. 'Didn't you try to get me back?' She felt tears press the back of her eyes.

Ben-Dad took a slow breath, as if the air had become heavy. 'I had no choice, Connie. It was agony, but I was so unwell. And once the courts had stopped me from seeing you, all I could do was write to you – at the airport, because they granted Mags's request not to give me her home address.

'How many letters did you write?' Connie waited for the answer: fifty, a hundred, five hundred?

He bit his top lip. 'Not letters, Connie. Cards. They were all I could manage, on your birthdays. From when you turned six and I'd come out of the coma.'

'You mean one birthday card a year?' A stone rose in her throat.

Ben-Dad sighed. 'I was still ill, on and off, for a long time. And even when I recovered, I thought you'd be too young to understand what had happened to me. Until, on your eleventh birthday, I plucked up the courage to write my first letter. Then, when you didn't answer—'

'I didn't get it!' A tear escaped down her cheek.

'I know that now. But at the time I thought it meant you didn't want anything to do with me.' He put a hand on the table. 'And I could understand why. So I didn't write again.'

Connie squeezed her fists in her lap. 'Didn't you guess Mags would block your letters?'

'She shouldn't have. I was legally allowed to write to you.' He gave a sad little snort. 'I knew she might, but I didn't dare to believe that could be the reason you hadn't replied. It was such a relief to hear it's true.' He drummed his hand on the table. 'And it makes sense. Maybe she was still angry with me for leaving you. Maybe she didn't really understand.'

'That you were sick? How could she not? It's pretty simple.' Connie found her hand reaching across the table. 'It wasn't your fault – Dad.' At last the word slipped out.

He tapped the top of her hand lightly. 'I'm sorry I didn't write more, but it took me ages to recover fully. Thank goodness I did, Connie. I've been completely well for a long time now. No blackouts or black moods. No visits to the doctor, let alone the hospit—'

'Over there!' squeaked a voice.

Holy Himalayas! Connie turned her head. That cleaner, Pruney Sue, was scuttling towards them, pointing her bony finger. Behind her came Thyo, then Abri. And behind them, with a face like a middle-aged T-rex, came Mags.

22. A Mammoth in Ice

'See?' Sue stopped at the café table with a grin like a rip in her face.

Mags pushed past Thyo and Abri.

'Get,' she panted at Dad. 'Away. From. Her.' She yanked Connie out of her seat and pulled her close. 'You're OK, love. It's OK.'

'Good job I was on Terminal 2 shift.' Sue's skinny eyebrows rose in expectation of thanks.

But Mags was too busy yelling. 'How dare you! My daughter's only twelve years old!'

Connie broke free from her arms. 'I'm not your daughter!' She ran behind her dad's chair.

'What?' Mags blinked at him. 'Who are you?' She stumbled backwards. 'Not ...' She clapped a hand to her mouth. 'It can't be. *You?* I didn't recognise ... your hair.'

He rose slowly from the chair. 'It's greyer. And thinner. Of course – it's been eight years.' He held out his hand.

Mags gained furious control. 'And more than six since you were banned from seeing Connie.'

'I know.' He spread his arms gently as if calming the air molecules. 'I'm sorry. It's just that Connie herself—'

'Sue.' Mags laced her fingers together and squeezed until the fingernails were white. 'Call security. Right now, please.' Her voice was the muted roar of a mammoth trapped in ice.

Sue skipped off like a happy schoolgirl.

Connie gripped the back of her dad's chair. 'I found his letter. And I asked him to come.'

'What?' Mags whispered. Cracks appeared in her glacier face.

A click broke the silence.

'Abri!' yelled Thyo behind her. 'Not now!' But it was too late. She'd taken out her phone and had caught them all: Dad with his arms outspread, Connie with hers now folded, and Mags, frozen in horror.

Abri looked at the picture. 'Perfect.'

Thyo whacked her arm. 'Idiot,' he hissed. 'You have no idea what's going on.' He turned to Connie. 'I'm sorry.

I saw them running through Arrivals.' He nodded at Mags and Sue. 'I guessed it was about you, so I followed. And so did she.' He thumped his sister again.

Connie glared at Mags. 'You came back too soon!'

Mags snorted. 'Well, I'm so sorry. Nice try with the egg. I was getting into the car when I remembered Maura's got a key.'

Dammit. Connie had forgotten the neighbour.

'I phoned and asked her to check the house. And guess what?' Mags widened her eyes in mock-surprise. 'You *hadn't* left the gas on. So I came back to work. Then Sue came up and said she'd seen you walk off with a stranger.'

'Please.' Dad raised his hands as if to block the death rays shooting from Mags's eyes. 'I understand why you're angry. But this was Connie's choice.'

'To meet my *dad*.' Connie pressed into the word. 'When I found out I *had* one.' Her voice wobbled. 'How could you lie to me for all these years?'

'I ...' Mags opened her mouth. But finding no answer inside, she blinked at Dad. 'Go,' she said quietly. 'Now.'

He took a step towards her. 'Please, hear me out, give me a chance to explain. I—'

He broke off as Sue reappeared with Joe in tow.

'I couldn't find a security guard,' Sue said sweetly, 'but I bumped into Joe.'

Connie guessed that 'bumping into' meant phoning him to say, 'So sorry to bother you, Joe, but there's been a bit of a scene, it's Mags and her girl again, could you spare a mo, seeing as you're the boss, and there's a man involved, and oh dear, poor Mags isn't having a good run is she, and what a pile of trouble she is, and wouldn't you pity anyone who got mixed up with her?'

'Joe – Mr Dooley,' said Mags. 'This man is hassling Connie.'

'This man,' said Connie, 'is my dad.'

Joe blinked from Mags to Dad then back again. 'So you're – married?'

'Of course not!' she snapped.

'He's the man-friend, then?'

'What are you on about? This man is no friend! And he has no legal rights. So if he doesn't go with you, I'm calling the police.'

'OK, OK.' Dad patted the air. 'I don't want trouble. I'll leave.'

'No!' Connie clutched his sleeve.

He pulled his arm gently away. 'I have to, Connie. She's right.' He turned to Mags. 'I know you don't care what I want,' he said softly. 'But what *Connie* wants is to see me again.' He reached into his jacket pocket. 'If you change your mind, here's my number.'

Mags snatched the card. 'The nerve of you!' She scrunched it up and threw it into a bin beside her. 'If you ever come here again,' she said icily, 'I'll see you in court.'

Joe stepped up and took Dad's arm. 'Come with me, please.' His voice was surprisingly firm. 'I'm escorting you out of the airport now.'

Mags nodded gratefully at Joe. As the two men turned to go, her whole body seemed to sag, as if it had a puncture.

'I'm sorry, Connie,' Dad said over his shoulder. 'So sorry.'

A sob rose in her throat. Turning to Mags she burst out, 'I hate you!'

— - —

They drove home in silence. Connie sat in the back, clutching Hue's box. Glancing at Mags's stony face in the rear-view mirror, she wanted to scream. But what good would that do? She settled for glaring silently out of the window.

Mags unlocked the front door. Connie marched past her and up the stairs. She heard the door slam and Mags shout, 'Where did you find that letter?'

Connie wheeled round on the landing, nearly knocking the house-phone off its little table. 'In your locker.'

'How dare you root about in my things!' Mags shouted up at her.

'How dare you hide my letter!' Connie yelled back down the stairs.

She waited for the *'Don't you speak to me like that,'* or the *'I can do what I like, missy!'* But it didn't come.

Instead Mags sat down heavily on a chair in the hall. 'I didn't know there *was* a letter. I thought it was just a card, like the others he'd sent every year.' She blinked up at Connie. 'I was going to give them to you when you're eighteen. They don't say much apart from happy birthday. I didn't even bother to open that one. I just thought it was more of the same.' She sighed. 'I was going to bring it home, add it to the pile. I thought I'd lost it.'

'It had slipped down the back of your locker.' Connie laughed bitterly. 'Thank goodness.'

Mags flinched. 'I hid them for your own good, Connie. I thought any contact, even a birthday card, might upset you. What if you wrote back and he never bothered replying? I couldn't bear you getting hurt. So I thought it was best you didn't know about him, not yet.' She tutted. 'There was no card this year. I thought he'd given up. And I was glad. How can he be trusted after what happened?'

'How can *you* be trusted?!' Connie squeezed the banister until the bones jutted on the backs of her hands. 'You had no right to open envelopes addressed to me. The court said he could write, and he did.'

'One sentence a year.' Mags snorted. 'Call that a loving father?'

'It wasn't his fault! He was ill and he's better now. He was explaining everything to me when you barged in.'

Mags put her hands on her knees. 'Look, Connie, however ill he was, however much it wasn't his fault, hasn't he proved how unreliable he is? I'm just trying to protect you.'

'And that's the problem!' Connie yelled. 'You're *always* trying to protect me. From going anywhere, from doing anything on my own. From slipping on rocks at the beach, from staying home by myself, from going on the Internet – when everyone else in the *world* does those things at my age!' She smacked the banister. 'And now you're protecting me from my own *family*. My *only* family!'

Mags dropped her eyes. 'I thought,' she said softly, 'that *I* was your family.'

Connie gave a little laugh, too old and cold for a twelve-year-old. 'You're just my prison guard.' She strode into her bedroom and slammed the door.

23. Saved by the Bin

Connie sank to her knees and put Hue's box on the floor of her bedroom.

'She says she's protecting me, but she's just protecting *herself!*' Sniffing back tears, she unclipped the lid. The top of Hue's knobbly head appeared, then his wary, wandering eyes. Connie reached in and lifted him out. 'She's scared I'll like Dad more than her.' She set him on the carpet. 'Well, breaking news, *I do.*'

Hue looked at her snootily, then began to prowl round the room, like a visiting aunt trying to guess the cost of the furniture.

There was a buzz from Connie's pocket. She fished out her phone.

```
Hey Connie. That sucked. You didn't
deserve it, nor did your dad. So I
```

```
thought you'd like my diary entry for
today. After you left, I got his card
from the bin. His number is 0044-707-
6251120. When Mags has calmed down,
come over to talk about the film. My
dad can collect you. Thyo
```

She punched the air. 'Yes!'

She texted back:

```
You're brilliant
```

But it wouldn't send. *Dammit*. She was out of credit. And she had a father to call. She opened the door and crept on to the landing. Grabbing the house-phone from the table, she went back into her room and closed the door quietly behind her.

'Hello?' came his voice almost immediately.

She felt a rush of warmth at his soft Yorkshire accent. An accent she could have – *should* have – had too.

'Hi, Dad.'

'Connie? How on earth did you—?'

'Thyo got your card for me. Out of the bin.'

'Wow!' He whistled down the phone. 'What a friend.'

'Yeah. Dad, I hate Ma—' She bit her lip. 'What Mags did.'

There was a pause. Then, 'It doesn't surprise me,' he said, almost wearily. 'Like I said, she's still angry with me. And I wonder if maybe she's also a bit ...' He trailed off.

'Jealous? 'Course she is. She's scared I'll like you more than her and want to come and live with you.'

'Wow, I'd love that, though the courts won't allow it yet, I'm afraid. But ...' Connie felt rather than heard the pause. 'What if you could just visit? Even for a day. If you came to Leeds, I could show you round, and explain properly what happened to me. You deserve to know.'

'That would be amazing. But you saw Mags. She'd never allow it.'

'No, I guess not.' He sighed. 'Well, I fly back tomorrow. If you find a free moment, when Mags is working and you can slip away, text me and maybe we can meet to say goodbye properly.' There was another pause. Then he said softly, 'I'm so glad you found me, Connie.'

When he'd rung off, she whispered into the mouthpiece, 'I love you, Dad.'

Slowly she replaced the receiver on the phone. A flat, grey ache settled in her stomach. That was it, then. No more Dad, at least not in person, until she was eighteen. And no more Thyo, at least not at the airport, to cheer her up.

Unless ...

An idea slid into her mind like a shark through water: neat, slick and huge.

No. I couldn't possibly.

She read Thyo's text again.

```
come over to talk about the film. My
dad can collect you.
```

'Except,' she murmured, 'I possibly could.'

Hue had crossed to the far wall and was beginning to climb the Northeast Ridge route (1995). Connie went over and lifted him gently off an outcrop. 'The problem is Mags.' She took him to his cage. 'How to get past her. We'll have to eat some humble pie, Hue.'

The look he gave her as she popped him on a branch said, 'Speak for yourself, sunshine.'

Mags was outside, pulling up weeds like a medieval dentist pulling teeth. Hearing Connie's footsteps she froze, bent over with her bottom stuck up in the air.

Connie took a deep breath. 'I'm sorry.'

Mags straightened up slowly. 'For what?' She pressed a hand to her back.

'Lying to you. Meeting my dad. Everything.'

Mags threw a thistle on to the lawn. 'I'm sorry too, Connie. I understand why you're so angry. But believe me, it's for your own good.'

'I know.' Connie chewed her lip. 'I was just so excited to see him, to know he was alive.'

Mags sat on a wooden bench beside the vegetable patch. 'I should've told you.' She pressed her fingers into her forehead. 'That was awful of me.'

'Well, yeah,' Connie said gravely, hoping to fan the flames of Mags's guilt. 'But it's OK.' She forced a smile. 'And to prove it, I'll buy you a house in Beverly Hills. I'm going to be a film star.'

Mags dropped her hands. 'What?'

Connie sat beside her. 'I didn't get a chance to tell you. The director wants me to be in that film with Thyo's family, because I helped them find a fossil yesterday.' She stopped. Better keep it vague. Explaining that she'd climbed a vertical cliff, and was going to do it again in front of the cameras, would hardly reassure Mags. And reassurance was crucial right now.

'You mean an interview? Wow, Con.' Mags nudged her arm. 'You'll be famous.'

Connie smiled. 'So I have to go to the site tomorrow morning.'

'Oh.' Mags frowned. 'But I can't take time off work.'

'You don't have to,' Connie said, in what she hoped was a breezy voice. 'Thyo said his dad will collect me from here. At nine,' she added. Mags would never let her stay home alone for long. 'And they've invited me to sleep over tomorrow night coz the filming takes two days. They'll drop me back the day after tomorrow. I'll call you when I know what time.'

'Whoa there.' Mags raised her hand. 'I don't think so.'

'Why not?' Connie forced her voice to stay calm. 'I'll be perfectly safe. You've met the family. You know them now.'

'Yes.' Mags shifted her bottom. 'But not after what's just happened, love.'

Connie was ready for this. 'Exactly. After what's just happened, the least you can do is give me some freedom. Like everyone else my age.'

Mags opened her mouth. But before she could answer Connie went on, 'And you know I'll be safe with the Miles family. Now's your chance to back off, let me have a bit of space.'

'But I ...' Mags picked at her teeth with a thumbnail. 'Well.' She took a long breath. 'I suppose ... Let me phone Naledi, then.'

Connie was ready for this too. 'Oh, come on!' She injected indignation into her voice. 'I'm not a baby. Ciara's mum never phones when she goes for sleepovers. Nor does anyone else's in my class. Please don't embarrass me. You can call me if you need me while I'm there.' Then she played her ace card. 'Just for once, be like a proper mum.'

Mags's eyelids fluttered. 'Oh,' she said quietly.

Connie couldn't look at her. She stared at the ground until, in an even quieter voice, Mags said, 'OK.'

Still not meeting her eyes, Connie said, 'Thank you. I'll phone Thyo and say you agree.' She stood up and hurried back to the house before Mags could change her mind.

Back in her bedroom, it wasn't Thyo she called, but her dad.

'Wow!' She heard him breathe out slowly. Then he said, 'That's an amazing idea. I'd never have thought of it, and I've got a PhD.'

She giggled.

'But I don't know, Connie. You shouldn't lie to Mags.'

Her stomach twisted.

'But then *she* shouldn't have lied to *you* all these years. And there's nothing I'd love more than to show you round Leeds. It's only one day. Good Lord, don't we deserve it?'

'We sure do.' She grinned all over the phone.

'My flight back is booked for tomorrow afternoon,' he said. 'I'll see if I can change my ticket to the morning and buy one for you.'

'Wait,' she said. 'Mags cleans in Terminal 1 Departures. What if she sees us?'

'Ah. Good point.' He paused. 'What about Aer Lingus? Hang on, I've got my computer here.' She heard a tapping sound. 'Yes! They fly from Terminal 2. And, hold on.' More tapping. 'Aer Lingus ... flights to Leeds, tomorrow.' More tapping, a bit of murmuring and, 'There's a flight at one o'clock. We have to be there two hours before. I could come and pick you up in a taxi – after Mags has gone to work.'

Her heart jumped as she gave him her address. 'We're about half an hour from the airport.'

'Wow,' he said. 'After all these years, I finally know where you live. I'll be there at ten-thirty. Remember to bring your passport. You'll need it to check in.'

'Park round the corner, Dad, in Elton Road. We've got a nosey neighbour. And what about the airport? What if Sue or Joe or anyone sees us again?'

'We'll just have to dive into the loo. Or wear false beards.'

Now she laughed, more from nerves than the joke.

When he'd rung off, a grin burst out of her. 'That was so easy, Hue.' One last piece and the jigsaw would be complete.

— · —

'*What?*' Thyo said down the phone, after she'd thanked him for retrieving her dad's number and told him her plan. 'I dunno, Connie, are you sure?'

'Why wouldn't I be?'

'Because you hardly know him.'

'He's my dad, Thyo.'

'But you've only met him twice.'

'I met him all the time until I was four.'

'And look what he did then.'

'He was sick. He's fine now. Plus, it's only a quick visit. Plus, all *you* have to do is pretend I'm with you if Mags asks, which she won't because she won't even see you. Plus, you're beginning to sound like her.'

'What? How can you say that? I'm the one who got you together in the first place, remember? I sent the email *and* met him off the plane when you were too scared. But you flying off with him behind Mags's back – that's a whole new barrel of nuts. What if she finds out?'

'She won't if you don't tell her!' Connie snapped. 'Promise you won't. Or anyone else. Because if you do ...' Her voice trembled. 'That's the end of our friendship.'

There was a pause. Then Thyo said in a flat voice, 'So what? I told you, I don't have any friends.'

'That's because you don't need them! Your mum's amazing, your dad's a sweetie and your sister loves you even though she pretends she doesn't. You've *got* a family; you've always had one. How can you try and stop me being with mine?'

'Connie, please, I'm not. I'm just saying you need to think it through a bit more.'

'*You're* the one who said thinking's overrated!' She slammed the phone down.

24. Passenger in a Pouch

Connie came down next morning to find Mags slicing cheese on the counter.

'Picnic,' she said, laying the pieces on buttered bread. 'For you and Thyo.'

'I'm sure the film crew will get us lunch.' Connie turned to the cereal cupboard, avoiding Mags's eyes.

'Snacks, then. You'll get hungry filming all day.' Mags wrapped the sandwiches in foil and put them in a lunch box.

'Thanks.' Connie crunched her cornflakes in time to the thump of her heart. 'You get ready for work. I'll clear up.'

And she did: stacking the dishwasher; sweeping the floor, and mopping it with a cloth on her hands and knees. Not because she felt bad about today, not at all, why should she? It would just be nice for Mags to come home to a clean floor.

Fifteen minutes later, Mags stuck her head round the door. 'I'm off then.' She came over and hugged Connie. 'Have a great time. I'll call you later, see how it's going.'

'No,' Connie said, pulling away. She might be on the plane with her phone off. And if she didn't answer, Mags would freak. 'I have to turn off my phone for the filming. I'll call you if there's a problem.'

Mags frowned, then chased it away with a smile. 'Ooh, listen to the movie star.' She kissed Connie's cheek. 'I'll want your autograph, mind.' She was clearly working very hard to seem relaxed.

Good, thought Connie.

When the front door had shut, she ran into the sitting room. Good job Mags was so organised; the top drawer in the corner desk was labelled 'Paperwork' and a folder inside said 'Passports'. Connie took hers out, last used on their only holiday abroad, two years ago, to Brittany, where it had rained all week and Mags had grumbled there was no Barry's tea.

Putting the passport in her hoodie pocket, she went into the hall and took down the key that hung by the front door. She let herself out and turned left along the road to the newsagent. (Thank goodness nosey Maura lived on the right.) She spent all her pocket money on phone credit so that she could call Mags tomorrow to say when Thyo's dad was bringing her home.

Back at the house, she took the lunch box from the kitchen up to her room. She stuffed it in a rucksack on top of the clean T-shirt, underwear and toothbrush she'd packed last night. She put the credit on her phone and the phone in her pocket. Then she tapped on Hue's cage. 'See you tomorrow.'

There was a rustle of leaves. A little blue head poked out.

'Mags will feed you in the morning,' said Connie. 'You'll be grand.' Hue crawled to the end of a branch. 'I'll be grand too.' He lifted a front leg and held it, stock-still, in the air. 'Why wouldn't I be?' She picked up the ruck-sack. 'Bye then.'

He crept to the front of the cage.

'What?' She spread her palm against the mesh.

He cocked his head.

'No way,' she said. 'They'd never let you on board.' She turned to go.

And stopped. She turned round again. 'I said no.'

He looked at her with one eye and at the wardrobe with the other.

'Unless,' she murmured, 'they didn't know.' She opened the wardrobe door. Hue's pillowcase pouch lay on a shelf.

— · —

At a quarter past ten she was sitting on the bottom stair with her notebook on her knee, the rucksack on her back and Hue on her front.

> **Hey Mags,**
> **I've taken Hue because Thyo's dad wants to**
> **look at him again before he starts drawing**
> **the dinosaur**

She paused, then added

> **for the film. It's going to be big. It might**
> **go to America.**

'Well it might,' she said, tearing off the sheet and leaving it on the bottom stair. And the more she used words like 'film' and 'big' and 'America', the more Mags's head might fill with stardom – and empty of suspicion.

The taxi was waiting half-way down Elton Road.

'Connie!' cried her dad, jumping out. And the strength of his hug and the joy in his face chased her nervousness away. 'Back to the airport, please,' he said to the driver. He sat beside Connie on the back seat and handed her her ticket, which he'd printed out. 'Terminal 2 Departures, Mags-free zone.' They high-fived.

They high-fived again at the airport when an official glanced at their passports and nodded them through like any normal dad and daughter, which, of course, they were, with their shared genes and surname; and which, of course, they weren't, with eight years and a million questions between them.

Connie slipped her passport back into her hoodie pocket and zipped it up. Now for the hard bit. *Keep still*, she begged Hue silently.

Dad took out a tray for the X-ray machine. 'Pop your rucksack on there,' he said, taking out another tray for his jacket and belt.

While her tray trundled slowly towards the machine, a lady in uniform beckoned her to the walk-through metal detector. Connie puffed out her hoodie. She could feel Hue squirm against her racing heart.

There was a beep as she went through the arch. No! Did it detect chameleons too? Her stomach squeezed tight.

'Don't look so worried, love.' The lady in uniform smiled. 'Are you wearing any jewellery?'

Connie breathed out. Of course. 'A locket.' She pulled it out.

The lady nodded. 'No problem.'

Connie tucked it back under her T-shirt and hoodie, her fingers shaking with relief.

Dad was putting his jacket back on. He looked up as she came to collect her rucksack from the tray. 'Everything OK?'

She nodded, placing a hand instinctively on her chest. Walking past the shops, she said, 'Could I get a bottle of water? I'm a bit thirsty.'

'Sure. Something to eat too?'

Her heart was still pounding. 'No, thanks, I'm not hungry. And Mags packed me sandwiches.'

'A hot chocolate, then? I fancy a coffee.' He pointed to a café ahead. 'And when you do feel like something to eat, I promise we'll do better than sandwiches.' Connie managed a smile. 'Why don't you get rid of them while I go and order?'

She found a bin and took out Mags's lunch box from her rucksack. And suddenly she *was* hungry, for a taste of the cheese, butter and bread that only Mags could get in the right proportions. She opened the lid, unwrapped the foil and bit off the corner of a sandwich. Dropping the rest in the bin, she felt as if she were throwing Mags away.

25. Partners in Mischief

'That beats soggy sandwiches,' said Dad, bringing a tray to the café table. 'Careful not to spill your hot chocolate. We don't want anyone getting burnt, do we?'

Connie blinked.

'Especially not anyone with cold blood.' He put the tray on the table. 'You know, I just saw the strangest thing. When you bent over the security belt to collect your rucksack, I could swear something poked out from the neck of your hoodie. Almost like a little head.'

Connie's hand flew to her chest.

Dad tutted. 'He won't make things easier, Connie.'

She opened her mouth. 'I ...' and closed it again.

'But he'll sure make them fun.' He put his hand in his back pocket. 'Won't he, Camelia?' His chameleon tie flashed red then blue then green.

Relief giggled through her. 'I thought,' she said shyly, 'that because you love chameleons, and you gave me Hue in the first place, you wouldn't mind him coming.'

'Connie Fuller.' He bowed in his chair. 'I am honoured, if a little inconvenienced, to be your partner in mischief.' He winked. 'Now, if you stay calm, hopefully Hue will too. We'll feed him when we get to Leeds. But you'll need to keep him hydrated. The air's very dry on a plane.'

'That's why I asked for a bottle of water just now.'

Dad whistled in admiration. 'You've really thought this through, haven't you? With any luck he'll sleep on the flight. A disco on your front might raise a few eyebrows.' His own eyebrows did a little dance, making his glasses wobble down his nose. Connie grinned. She bent down to her rucksack, leaning against her chair. Unzipping a side pocket, she took out a small plastic tube with a spray nozzle and filled it with water from the bottle Dad had bought. 'All ready,' she said, putting it back in the rucksack. She sat up and reached for her mug of hot chocolate. 'Oh.' Her hand stopped.

'You OK?' said Dad. 'What's wrong?'

'Nothing.' She tried not to look at the mini-marshmallows on top. But still a sickness slithered up her throat, an echo of the first – and last – time she'd eaten them. She tasted again their pale, slimy sweetness, pictured the pattern on the table as she'd spat them out all those years ago.

Now, with a spoon, she scooped them on to the saucer.

'Oh, don't you like marshmallows? Sorry.'

'It's fine,' she said, amazed at the strangeness of memory: how a shared moment, eight years ago, could be forgotten by him but stay in her mind so clearly that the taste punched back into her mouth.

She pushed the saucer away. 'Dad, what was my … what was Mum like?'

He brought his cup to his lips and took a tiny sip of coffee. 'Like you.'

'You don't know me!' She bit her cheek. She hadn't meant to sound so sharp.

He put his cup down. 'I mean, she looked like you. From the moment you were born, you were the spit of her. That's why we called you Connie – constant – a continuation of her. And also because we were so happy, we didn't want anything to change.'

So that explained her frilly maid's cap of a name. *I must tell Thyo*, she thought. There was a sting in her chest. *If he ever speaks to me again.*

'But now I know,' Dad said, 'that the only constant thing *is* change.'

'Do you ... do you have a photo of her?'

'No.' He looked down and fiddled with a teaspoon. 'I find it hard to ... they're all in a box in my attic.'

Idiot, Connie cursed herself. *Now I've ruined things.*

But he puffed out a breath like a weightlifter about to raise a bar and said, 'Your mum loved salt and vinegar crisps. Musicals. The colour turquoise. And mountain hikes. Maybe that's where you get your climbing from. She wasn't a rock-climber, but she skipped up mountain paths like a goat. She'd be so proud to know you're going to climb Muchu Chhish.'

Going to, not *want to*. And he'd even remembered the name! Connie's heart felt too big for her chest.

'And she loved hot chocolate. *With* marshmallows. That must be why I got it wrong.' He looked up. 'You remind me of her so much.'

For the first time it struck Connie that their reunion must be just as hard for him. 'Is that good?' she said softly.

He gave a sad-happy smile. 'The best.'

26. A Businessman of a City

The flight went as smoothly as it could for a girl with a chameleon on her chest sitting next to a father she hadn't seen for two-thirds of her life. There was only one awkward moment, when Connie peeked down her hoodie, saw Hue's dull brown, dehydrated head, and sprayed water on him.

'Drinks, sandwiches, snacks?' A flight attendant stopped by their row. Seeing the damp patch spreading across Connie's front, his eyebrows bunched together like colliding caterpillars.

'My daughter spilt her water,' said Dad, not missing a beat. 'Could you possibly get a towel?'

As the attendant glided off, Dad and Connie fist-bumped. It was wicked and brilliant to conspire with him, to share secrets and break rules like Mags never did.

Gazing down on the clouds, Connie felt a soaring inside, like a kite cutting free from its rope, lifting her high above order, routine and the stifling love of a woman whose claim on her was nothing but legal.

Well, almost nothing. There was the bedroom Mags had paid for. The birthday parties. The hugs when Connie was sad or sick or fell over. The march into school to tell Mrs Farrell that actually it was Billy Kerr who'd copied Connie in the maths test, not the other way round. The home-made pizza, the banoffee pie and those perfect cheese sandwiches.

As the plane touched down, doubt was nibbling the edges of her excitement. Nobody knew where she was except a scribble-haired boy she'd fallen out with. What if she had an accident, or fell sick? She found herself slipping her hand into Dad's.

He smiled in surprise. 'Welcome to Leeds, Connie.' Still holding her hand, he led her through the airport to the car park where he'd left his car while he flew to Dublin.

Holy Himalayas, a BMW! She slid on to the sleek front seat. *He's rich.* Would that mean an end to charity-shop coats? Surely, at the very least, he'd send her a clothes allowance. Hey, maybe he'd pay for her to go to Glenview College with Ciara next term – or even take her on holiday to Tenerife to stay in that fancy hotel with its tiny bottles of bubble bath!

The car purred through mist into grey Leeds. And boy was it grey. Grey sky, grey roads, tall grey buildings. It all looked so smart and efficient: a businessman of a city compared to the warm-hearted granny of Dublin. Even the raindrops were neater, glittering down the car window in orderly lines.

'So, here's the plan,' Dad said. 'We'll get some lunch and spend the afternoon in the city centre. Then we'll grab dinner and head over to my office so I can show you what I do. And then we'll go home. I live a bit of a way out.'

'Why can't we go to your work now?'

Dad looked steadily at the road ahead. 'Our research is ground-breaking, Connie, and highly sensitive.' His voice was serious. 'We're not supposed to let anyone in without security clearance. I guess the idea is to stop competitors who might steal our ideas. No fear of that with you, of course. But just in case anyone at work asks questions, it's best to leave it till later when it'll be quieter.'

'But it was your idea for me to visit.'

He raised a hand. 'I know. And it's fine. Rules are there to make people do the right thing. And the right thing, in this case, is to show you my work. I told you I study chameleons. Well, I think you'll be fascinated. The project I'm working on is incredibly exciting. It could uplift millions of lives. I can't explain it now, but wait till I show you. You'll be blown away.'

A thrill ran through Connie. He was clearly so clever and his work so important and valuable – a million miles from the carboard researching she'd imagined!

'Anyway,' he said, 'a few hours in Leeds will give me a chance to buy you a present. And talking of rules, here's one for you: I've got eight birthdays to catch up on, so you're absolutely not allowed to worry about the price.'

'Thanks.' She smiled, then paused, pretending that she had to think about it. 'Well, there is something I'd love.' She added cheekily, 'Mags won't buy me one,' hoping that would sway him.

But when she told him, it did the opposite. 'Ahh.' He drew a little breath. 'Sorry, Connie, but I have to agree with Mags on this. Part of our research at Mexel Mann looks at the effect of phone radiation on young people's brains. We've found that under the age of fourteen, phone waves can do a lot of damage.'

'Really? All phones – even basic ones?'

He nodded. 'People your age really shouldn't be using any sort of mobile device.'

She fingered her pocket. Thank goodness she hadn't mentioned her stupidphone. She couldn't bear his disapproval.

They had lunch in a posh pizzeria with booths where she could sneak some lettuce for Hue from Dad's side salad. Then they went shopping. She chose a pair of blue Nike trainers that cost a hundred and three whole pounds, which she knew was even more in euros. Trying them on felt like stepping on giggles. 'Could I wear them now?' she asked.

Dad laughed. 'Just like me. If I buy new shoes, I always want to wear them out of the shop.'

Connie smiled in wonder at this shared habit, a reminder of their shared genes. Dad gave her a hundred and ten pounds – in cash! – to pay for them at the counter. When she came back with the change, he waved his hand and said, 'Keep it.'

Connie looked at the five-pound note and two-pound coin, chunkier and more important-looking than euro coins. 'Really?' It somehow felt like a fortune. 'Thank you,' she said shyly, slipping the money into the front pocket of her jeans.

'Pleasure. I know you can't spend it in Ireland, but it's a souvenir of our day.'

Souvenir. The word Thyo had used. She felt a nip of guilt as his face grinned into her mind. Hot on its heels came a burst of triumph. She shouldn't have yelled at him; he was only trying to help. But look how wrong he'd been. She was having the time of her life. And yes, she would treasure the money as a true souvenir, a memory that would become part of her.

'Or you can use it next time you come over.' Dad patted her shoulder. 'Keep it as an incentive, a promise that you'll return.'

'Thanks, Dad.' Connie hugged him.

She bounced through the afternoon, trying to wear in her new trainers so that, when she got back, she could convince Mags that Abri had passed them on. It wasn't easy to find any dirt on the gleaming floor of the shopping mall, but she managed to step on a piece of chewing gum that stuck to her sole, and to scuff her toes against a rubbish bin. In another shop she tried on a jacket, slipping into it over her hoodie so that Hue would stay hidden. He squirmed a little but then settled down, which was a sign, Dad said, that she should have it.

They went to a bookshop where she chose a book called *At Their Peak*, about famous mountaineers, and a notebook with dinosaurs on the cover. 'For Thyo,' she said, hoping silently that he'd accept her peace offering.

When there was no room in her rucksack for more presents, they went to a restaurant for dinner. Awed by the sleek waiters and smartly folded serviettes, she followed Dad's lead and ordered lasagne, even though she was still full from lunch.

'I just need the loo,' she said. Sitting in a cubicle, she took out her phone from her hoodie pocket and texted.

```
Hey Thyo, I'm sorry for yelling at you.
I was just scared you'd ruin things.
I'm in Leeds and it's brilliant. Dad's
```

so cool and kind and he's bought me
loads of stuff. How are you? Have they
identified the fossils yet?

Please forgive me, she begged, pressing SEND.

A text came back as she was washing her hands.

Hi Connie. Sorry too. I'm really glad
it's going well. And don't worry, I
haven't told anyone. Everyone's happy
with the mother and nest theory. And
guess what - Ma thinks it's a NEW
species, which is why she couldn't
identify it!

Relief swept through her. 'Yes!' She pulled out her hoodie neck and kissed the top of Hue's head, ignoring his little wriggle of distaste. 'He's over it, Huey.'

Thanks. And wow, a new dinosaur!
Got to go now.

If only she could tell Dad that she'd helped to discover a dinosaur! But then he'd ask questions, and she might let slip that Thyo had just texted. And even if she didn't, Thyo might text again, or Mags might call, and Dad would find out that Connie was damaging her under-fourteen-year-old brain with a phone. So she turned it off and zipped it safely in her hoodie pocket.

She returned to the table as the waiter arrived with their food.

'Ooh, these look good.' Dad grinned. 'Well chosen, us.' He picked up a jug from the table and filled Connie's glass with water. 'So.' He filled his own glass. 'We'll head to my office after this, then home. We have to be at the airport at eight o'clock tomorrow morning. The flight's at ten. I'll fly with you, see you safely to Dublin, then put you in a taxi. You should be home by midday.'

'But Mags doesn't get home till about two. And she doesn't let me stay home alone.'

'Really?' Dad tilted his head in surprise.

Heat rushed up Connie's neck. Fussy, embarrassing, mollycoddling Mags.

'Well, no problem.' He smiled. 'We'll sneak out of the airport, take a taxi into Dublin and find something fun to do. I'll see you safely home for whatever time you want to be back with Mags. Then I'll catch the next flight home.'

Back with Mags. Connie picked up her fork and stabbed her lasagne. Those were three words she didn't want to think about right now.

27. Chameleons

The evening sky glowed pink and orange as they drove to Dad's office.

'We're heading into the city centre,' he said.

The traffic became heavier, the pavements busier. People in grey coats rushed along grey pavements past grey shops and office blocks.

They turned left into a road lined with tall buildings. Half-way down, Dad slowed and turned left again. He pulled up in front of a barrier. Behind it was a car park and, behind that, a gleaming metal tower. Dad opened the car window and tapped numbers into a keypad. As the barrier rose, Connie gazed at the tower. It stuck up like a silver tooth between lower, flat-roofed neighbours. Across the front of the tower, near the top, was a sign in huge letters:

 MEXEL MANN SOLUTIONS

Connie recognised the logo from Dad's letter, which she still had in her back pocket. She gave it a grateful pat. If it hadn't been for that single sheet of paper, she wouldn't be here now.

So why, as Dad parked in front of a workplace that spoke of his brilliance and wealth, did she feel a sudden urge to be sitting on the sofa with Mags, watching *Bake Off* and eating home-made brownies?

'Cool,' she said stupidly, feeling very uncool indeed in the middle of this strange city where everything, from the road signs to the dogs on leads, looked busy and important and somehow in charge.

'You can leave your rucksack in the car,' Dad said. 'We've got everything Hue needs inside.'

She followed him across the car park, empty apart from the BMW, to the curved entrance doors. They squashed her reflection like a mirror in a funfair. She looked away, feeling even less cool.

Dad tapped another keypad on the wall. The doors hummed apart. A light came on as they walked into a large entrance lobby. On the left stood a white reception desk, an island in a sea of blue carpet. Soft music played in the background. Somehow it made Connie think of Mrs Farrell who, when she got cross, went quiet, as if to shame the class into behaving themselves, which only made them misbehave more.

'What do you do here?' she asked. 'I mean, I know the mobile phone stuff, but what else?'

'All sorts,' Dad said. 'Everyone's caught up in their own research. To be honest, we don't really know much about each other's projects.' He pressed the lift button on the wall. 'You can take off your hoodie if you like. No-one's around.'

Connie pulled it over her head, careful not to knock Hue or snag her locket, and tied it round her waist. The chameleon's eyes rolled everywhere, taking in the surroundings.

The lift pinged its arrival. They went in, and Dad pressed a button. As they rose, Hue froze in his pouch, staring at the mirrored lift wall in front. 'He's seen his reflection,' said Connie. Hue hissed and turned bright orange.

Dad laughed. 'He thinks it's another chameleon. I told you they're dim.'

Connie cupped her hand protectively over the pouch. 'I don't think that's dim. I mean, if you didn't know about mirrors, you'd think it was another person staring back at you.'

'Fair point.' He nodded. 'And maybe Hue's grumpy with hunger too. Let's get him some dinner.'

They came to the fourth floor. Across more blue carpet was a metal door. Dad took out a card from his pocket and tapped it against the handle.

It's like being inside a spaceship, Connie thought: *all metal and beeps and doors that open with cards.*

They entered a big, brightly lit room. Around the walls stood cages on stands. They were tall and narrow, filled with dense foliage that whirred with the sound of insects. In the middle of the room was a table with a chair tucked underneath. On top stood a desk lamp and a tray. The air was damp, heavy and super-warm. Every now and then a leaf inside a cage shivered with the drip of water, or the leap of an insect, or ...

'Chameleons!' Connie spotted a blue head in a cage on the left. Then a pink tail on the right, uncoiling slowly from a branch.

'Twenty-five,' Dad said. 'One in each cage. As you know, they're not exactly sociable. If we put two together, they'd fight.'

Hue was fidgeting in his pouch, energised by the warm, bright air. 'Can I let him out?' she asked.

'Of course,' said Dad. 'He's earned a holiday after that trip. And this room is a five-star chameleon hotel.' He went over to the table. 'So we'd better get him a five-star meal.'

As Connie lifted Hue out of the pouch and set him gently on the floor, Dad pulled out a drawer beneath the table. He took out a glass jar and unscrewed the lid that was punctured with airholes. Turning it upside down, he emptied a cricket on to his palm. It buzzed across the room and landed on the door of a cage on Connie's left. It perched there, as still as an origami model.

Not for long. Hue's tongue flicked out. And the next second he was crunching contentedly on the poor creature.

Dad released another cricket from the jar. 'That should keep him busy for a bit,' he said, going to a cage on Connie's right. 'Because I've got something to show you that will change your life.'

28. P7

Dad lifted a latch and opened the door of the cage. He laid his hand on a branch inside. For a few seconds nothing happened. Then a dark blue head poked out between leaves. A chameleon emerged and placed one dainty foot, then another, on the back of Dad's hand. Then another and another, and now Dad was walking across to the table with the chameleon perched on his arm.

In the middle of the floor, Hue stopped munching. Glaring up at his rival, he puffed out his body. The blue-green stripes on his back flared to orange. The chameleon on Dad's arm hissed. Hue turned his back and continued eating.

'Drama queens the lot of them.' Dad laughed. 'Calm down, P7.'

'Who?' said Connie, frowning.

'Not as imaginative as Hue, I know,' Dad said, 'but the names help us keep track. P7 is the seventh panther chameleon we've had at Mexel Mann. V5 – in that cage on your right – that's our fifth veiled cham. They're the oldest ones here. Then there's P8, P9, and V6, V7 and so on.'

Strange, she thought. *He names his tie Camelia, but real chameleons just get letters and numbers.*

'What happened to the others?' she asked. 'P1 to P6 and V1 to V4?'

'Old age.' Dad lifted P7 off his arm. 'Or accidents.' He lowered the chameleon on to the tray on top of the table.

'What do you mean "accidents"?' A wire of unease twisted in her chest.

'Connie.' Dad looked up at her, his hand resting gently on P7's back. 'Will you promise me something?'

She swallowed. 'What?'

'For the next few minutes, don't judge anything. Just trust me until I've finished. Can you do that?'

She nodded, putting her hands on the top of the cold steel chair-back. Her throat felt dry.

Dad gestured for her to sit down. As she pulled the chair out, he turned back to the table. He lifted two canvas straps, one attached to each side of the tray, and clipped them together over the chameleon's little neck. He clipped two more tray straps over P7's back and two more over his tail. They were loose enough to be comfortable but firm enough to keep P7 – *Peter*, Connie renamed him silently – in place.

Dad reached in the drawer beneath the table. He brought out a plastic box, opened the lid and took out what looked like a Tic Tac mint: a white oval the size of his thumbnail. He put it on the table in front of Peter. The blue and yellow stripes on his back became stronger.

'Those deepening colours show that he recognises this chameleon egg. He feels protective.'

'Is he the dad, then?'

'Yes.'

Connie suddenly thought of the dinosaur fossils back in Ireland. Naledi had assumed it was a mother protecting the eggs. Why not a father? She must remember to ask when she got back.

She looked at Peter's colourful display. 'So he knows that tiny white thing is a future chameleon,' she said, 'even though it looks nothing like one. And he cares about it. See? I told you they're smart.'

Dad smiled. 'I'd agree with you, if they learned all that. But it's just instinct. They're born with it – pre-programmed if you like. They don't think it up for themselves.'

Connie pursed her lips. Wasn't it smart to be born with a desire to protect your young? So smart that you didn't have to waste time learning it? Surely Dad, with his track record as a parent, should admire that. Why did humans always look down on other animals? Especially ones with scales and claws that went round minding their own business, instead of ruining the planet with factories and fracking and wet wipes.

'What *is* amazing,' Dad said, reaching into the drawer again, 'is the way chameleons show their feelings. Literally. That's why we use them at Mexel Mann. Males, because they have stronger colours. The females we use just for breeding.'

Use? Connie didn't like that word.

Dad brought out a little silver tool from the drawer. 'Now, ready? Watch this.'

She'd just realised that it was a hammer when—

'No!' she shrieked as the egg smashed into a thousand pieces. Peter flooded a dark, distressed grey.

Connie stared at Dad. 'What? How could you ...?' The words drained away. He held up a hand. 'Remember,' he said steadily, 'don't judge. Not yet.' He put the hammer back in the drawer. 'I promise it'll be OK.' He reached out to pat her shoulder. Connie shrank away. She looked round for Hue. He'd climbed through the open door of Peter's cage and was nibbling a leaf inside. His colours were bright enough. Did that mean he hadn't seen what Dad had done? Or that he had but – as Dad would no doubt say – his hunger instinct was stronger than his caring instinct, so that the joy of a juicy leaf outweighed the pain of seeing another chameleon's egg being smashed? She'd never have thought that until now. But Dad was so clever, and so OK with this, and it was all so confusing, and it had been such a big day, and ...

'I promise,' Dad said again gently, 'P7 will be fine in a few minutes.'

Connie blinked back tears. 'But the egg won't.'

Dad waved his hand. 'Don't worry. It might well have been infertile. And even if it wasn't, we have hundreds more. Our females are great producers.'

Producers? Connie felt sick. *You mean mothers.*

The chameleon squirmed in his straps, still miserably grey.

'Let's cheer you up, P7,' Dad said, more like a friendly doctor than a lizard murderer. He reached into the drawer again and brought out a slice of apple. He put it at the end of the table, about ten centimetres from the chameleon's head. Peter's eyes skittered between the food and Dad. Then his tongue shot out, snatched the apple and brought it to his mouth. Slowly the grey on his back softened to blue.

'He's recovering,' Dad said, placing three slices of carrot by the apple. As Peter munched, blue and yellow stripes reappeared on his back. 'See? All better. I'd leave him longer, but I want to show you that everything really is OK.'

He brought out the hammer again from the drawer and held it in front of Peter.

'No!' Connie yelled.

'Don't worry,' said Dad. 'I'm not going to do anything this time. But look at P7. What does that tell you?'

Peter had flooded dark grey again.

'He's upset,' said Connie with a vehemence that showed Peter wasn't the only one. 'He remembers that hammer and what you did with it.'

'Exactly.' Dad returned the hammer to the drawer. 'Now this is where the fun begins.'

Fun? Connie couldn't look at him. So instead she stared at his hands as they reached for the desk lamp on the table. He slid it across to Peter. He bent the metal stalk of the lamp until the domed shade sat over the chameleon's head. He pressed a switch on the base of the lamp.

'Now we wait for a minute.' Dad pointed to a clock on the wall.

'What are you doing to him?' Connie's voice was full of sawdust. 'Will he be OK?'

'I promise,' Dad said.

The second hand lurched round the clock face. Connie turned to look at Hue again. He perched on a branch in Peter's cage with his back turned, happily oblivious.

At last Dad turned off the switch. Peter had relaxed completely into his resting colours: a blue and yellow back, pinky-red legs and darker blue head. Dad pushed the lampshade away.

'Watch this.' He brought out the hammer from the box again and held it in front of Peter's face. The lizard eyed it lazily. 'What do you see?'

'Nothing,' Connie said. 'I mean, he hasn't changed colour.'

'Exactly!' Dad gave a clap. 'Which means he's absolutely happy. He doesn't remember a thing about that hammer or what it did.'

'But before you put that thing over his head, he did.' Connie stared at the machine. 'What did it do to him?'

Dad patted the lampshade. 'It modified the limbic system of P7's brain.'

'The what?'

'It's an area below the medial temporal lobe of the cerebrum. It's made up of the hippocampus, the amygdala and the neocortex.'

Connie's face must have shown that she only understood the words with less than six letters because Dad said, 'Sorry.' At last he seemed to realise he wasn't talking to a brain surgeon. 'To put it simply, this machine just wiped a memory.'

29. Mimi

Connie stared in bewilderment at the desk lamp. 'It wiped his memory?' she repeated.

At least she thought she did. But Dad shook his head. 'It wiped a memory. Big difference. If all his memory were removed, P7 wouldn't remember that carrot is a food.' Peter was nibbling away in multi-coloured contentment. 'No, it targets a specific memory then removes it for ever. It's a Modified Individual Memory Inhibitor. Or, as I call it, Mimi.' He patted the lamp. 'It's taken six years to develop. You could say it's my other child.' He smiled. 'Connie, say hello to your little sister Mimi.'

Connie met his smile with stone. *He's done it again – named a machine but not an animal.*

'How?' She swallowed. 'I mean, how does it know *which* memory to remove?'

'Mimi picks up the memory that's causing the most negative response when the light goes on, and zaps it.' Dad snapped his fingers. 'Gone!' He lifted Peter from the table on to his arm. 'That's why this little guy wasn't upset when he saw the hammer the third time. He didn't connect it with the egg smashing because he didn't *remember* the egg smashing.' He carried Peter back to his cage. The chameleon sat on his arm, still a relaxed blue and yellow, pink and red. 'See? I told you he'd be fine.'

Connie followed him. 'But he wasn't fine when you smashed it.'

'I know it was hard to watch,' said Dad. 'But, I promise you, P7 is perfectly OK now.'

There was a flurry of leaves in the cage. Hue emerged from the undergrowth and perched on a branch. Seeing Peter on Dad's arm, Hue opened his jaws and hissed. Peter's back blazed orange as he faced the cage-crasher.

Connie reached inside and removed Hue before things could get nasty. 'How does the machine' – no way could she call it Mimi – 'find the most negative memory to zap?' She cradled Hue in her arms.

Dad popped Peter on to a branch. The chameleon turned and vanished into the foliage. 'The science is complicated, but I can try and simplify it. Let's go to my office.'

Connie's head swirled with questions as she followed him to the door. *How do you cut out a single memory? Why would you? And what's it got to do with you walking away eight years ago?*

Dad took the card from his pocket and tapped the door handle. The door beeped open. With Hue on her shoulder, Connie followed him down the corridor. Their shoes whispered on the thick carpet. They stopped at another door. A sign on the front read 'Head of Research' in gold letters. Dad beeped the door with his card again.

So much security, even inside. Since entering the chameleon room, Connie had tensed up, as if someone had tightened the screws on her muscles, and all this tapping and beeping didn't help. What a place for Dad to spend his days! She glanced at his photo on the card. He wasn't wearing glasses and had a beard that made his face look fuller and rounder, somehow more at ease. Whatever he said about his work being fine, it had clearly taken a toll on him.

'How long have you been at Mexel Mann?' she asked as he opened the door.

'Longer than you've been alive, love.'

It was the first time he'd used that word. And it should have been – well, lovely. But since he'd smashed the egg, a crack had formed in the tower of her respect. Now it felt as if he were trying to win back her favour. When Mags called her 'love' – which was all the time – it felt natural and effortless, almost like Connie's second name.

Dad's office was neat and spare. There were white walls and a desk with drawers, a swivel chair and a computer on top. In one corner was a filing cabinet and, in the other, a grey armchair. Hue crept down from Connie's shoulder and set about exploring. He high-stepped across the carpet towards the only green in the room: a plant on the desk with smooth, shiny leaves.

'Devil's ivy,' she murmured, recognising it from Hue's cage at home.

Dad nodded. 'For the chams to munch. I sometimes bring one in for observation. Have a seat.' She went to the armchair while he sat at the desk.

'So.' He opened the top drawer. 'How did Mimi do it – remove one single memory from P7?' He took out a pen and a sheet of paper. On the left he drew a little house: a square with a triangle on top. Below it he wrote:

Hippocampus –
storehouse of memory

'Every time you remember an event, it's as if there's an explosion in the storehouse. Electrical pulses carry the memory along nerves.' He drew an arrow from the hippocampus, left to right across the page. Underneath it he wrote:

Nerve carrying
the memory

'Say the nerve ends here.' He ended the arrow. 'And another one starts here.' He left a gap and then drew a second arrow. 'This gap between the nerves is called a synapse. When the memory gets to the end of the first nerve, it jumps on to special chemicals called neurotransmitters. They carry it across the gap, like tiny ferry boats.' He drew little dots in the gap. Underneath he wrote

Neurotransmitters
carry memories
across the synapse

'This is where it gets interesting,' he said, 'because each neurotransmitter carries a specific memory. So how could you block a specific memory?'

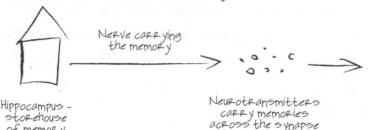

Nerve carrying
the memory

Hippocampus –
storehouse
of memory

Neurotransmitters
carry memories
across the synapse

Connie stared at the picture. The lines and blobs danced before her tired eyes. 'By stopping its ferry – the neuro-transmitter – from crossing the gap?'

Dad clapped. 'There's my super-smart girl!'

The answer had seemed pretty obvious, but still Connie felt a surge of pride.

'There's a gas called xenon,' he said, 'that does exactly that. It attaches to the strongest memory triggered at that moment. Remember that lampshade on Mimi?'

She nodded.

'Well, the light inside contains xenon gas. There's a hole in the bulb. When I switched Mimi on, xenon flowed out and was inhaled by P7. It entered his brain and found the neurotransmitter carrying the bad memory of the egg-smash. Then it blocked it. So the memory was removed from P7's mind. It's as if it never happened.'

'The egg never smashed,' Connie murmured.

'Precisely.' Dad's foot tapped excitedly against the leg of his chair.

'But there wouldn't have been a bad memory in the first place if you hadn't smashed the egg,' she said.

'I know. I had to organise that, to show you.' He swivelled round in his chair. 'Unfortunately, though, we can't always organise our lives.' He wrapped his right hand round his left fist. 'Things happen beyond our control. Bad things, that leave painful memories. And sometimes those memories can mess up the rest of our lives. Think of earthquakes and fires and floods. Think of soldiers haunted by war. Think of a man,' he said softly, 'who couldn't get over the death of his wife.'

30. Jigsaw Pieces

While Dad was talking, Hue had climbed the leg of the desk. Connie watched him walk across to the plant pot and nibble a low-hanging leaf. She knew she should say, 'It was an accident, Dad; Mum's death wasn't your fault.' But her tongue had dried up like mud in the sun.

'I couldn't bear it.' Dad pressed his fists together. 'Not just the grief, but the guilt of driving that car. I had to stop the pain. For myself and also for you.' He stared at his lap. 'The strange thing was,' he murmured, 'I'd been studying this very subject. And so had your mum.'

'She was a scientist too?'

'A psychologist like me. She had a wonderful mind, and an even more wonderful heart. She hated seeing people unhappy. She always said, "If your fear hasn't happened, it's imaginary, and if it has happened, it's over.

The future and the past are fiction. The only reality is now."'

Connie thought of meeting Thyo last week and of secondary school next term, of dinosaurs roaming millions of years ago, and of returning to Mags tomorrow. Were they all just stories in her head?

'We met as researchers at Mexel Mann,' Dad said, 'trying to find a way to remove bad memories. Pretty early on we found out how to remove all memory, by disabling the hippocampus. The hard part was how to target a specific memory. We did test after test.'

'On chameleons?' Connie said sharply. 'Mum was OK with that?'

'Not exactly.' Dad reached out to squeeze her hand, but Connie pulled it away. He sighed. 'She loved animals, but she loved humans more. She wanted to help people in pain.' He ran his hand over his cheek. 'We tried electric currents, lasers, drugs, all sorts. At first the chameleons' colour changes showed they'd lost all memory. Then some memories, but randomly and only temporarily. Then ...' He shook his head. 'Then your mum died. And I was in so much pain, I couldn't wait for the science to catch up. So I experimented on myself, using the latest pill we'd developed. But, as you know, I started having blackouts and forgetting things.'

'Like your own daughter.'

He rubbed his temple. 'The science didn't work then, Connie. That's why we moved from the pills to xenon gas. And that does work – perfectly – as you saw with P7.'

Connie pressed her palms on the arms of the chair. 'He's a chameleon. How do you know it works on humans?'

'Because we've tested it.' He was about to say more when he tapped his forehead with the heel of his hand. 'Ah! You know what, I forgot to close P7's cage.'

Connie frowned. 'I thought I saw you do it.'

'I didn't pull the bolt across. He could get out.'

'Does that matter? It's safe in there, isn't it? Hue was wandering around OK.'

'Yes, with us there to watch him.' Dad stood up from the desk. 'But there's a window above the cages and I'm pretty sure it was open. You know what great climbers they are. He could easily get up there. And not even a cham would stand a chance four floors up a building with sheer metal walls. I won't be long.' He went out.

Connie sat very still. Dad had added new camera angles to the eight-year-old movie she'd replayed so often in her mind. She gazed ahead and let the scene in the airport unfold through his eyes. Getting up to fetch her another hot chocolate; standing at the bar; talking to Mags; going to the bathroom; taking a pill; wandering out in oblivion, and then blacking out completely. How broken-hearted he must have been: how lonely, scared and confused. It was all so desperately sad and strange. No wonder he'd wanted her to come here to understand his story. He could never have explained it in writing.

Although ... hadn't there been something in that letter – a little hint of his mental state? 'What was that phrase he used, Huey?' she said, looking across at the desk. Hue had finished eating and was wandering towards the computer. Connie took out Dad's letter from her back pocket. She'd read it so many times over the last few days that the fold lines were furry and frail. Carefully she spread it on her lap. She scanned the sheet. There, half-way down:

that moment when I lost my mind. Literally.

'Literally,' she murmured. She'd glossed over it before – there was so much else she hadn't understood – but now the words burned into her. His poor mind, literally lost, to grief and that untested medication.

Whatever the damage to his brain, though, he was still the smartest person she'd ever met. She looked at his diagram on the desk. If his mind was still so amazing after all that meddling, imagine what it must have been like before he'd taken the—

Wait. She frowned at the diagram.

> Neurotransmitters
> carry memories
> across the synapse.

Then at the letter on her lap.

> I've paid ever since for that moment when

Then back at the diagram.

> Hippocampus –
> storehouse of memory

'The writing,' she murmured. 'It's different, Hue.'

As if to say, 'So what?' he turned his back and lifted his tail. A shiny dark blob dropped on to the desk.

'Oh no!' Dad really wouldn't appreciate poop on his perfect white work surface. Connie looked round for something to wipe it up. Not Dad's diagram; she hadn't finished with that. Maybe there was a box of tissues. She stood up, laid Dad's letter on the chair and went over to the desk. Inside the top drawer she found a stapler, a hole punch, some pens and a textbook entitled *Brain-waves: Understanding neural pathway*s. Beneath the book was an envelope, opened across the top. She could remove the letter inside and use the envelope to wipe up the poop. She took it out and read the address.

> **James Casey, Head of Research**
> **Mexel Mann Solutions**
> **12–14 Merton Street**
> **Leeds LS2 8JH**

She bit her lip. *James Casey?* Wasn't Dad the head of research? That's what it said on the door, so that's what she'd assumed. Unless he was using James Casey's office, of course. Before she had time to decide that the letter was none of her business, she took it out.

Medi-Devices Inc.
P.O. Box 4165
San Francisco
CA 98774

James Casey
Head of Research
Mexel Mann Solutions
12–14 Merton St
Leeds LS2 8JH
UK

14th April

James,

In reply to your request for more time, I refer to our business contract. Volunteers are your responsibility. Unless product safety is proved by the agreed date, we cannot proceed with manufacture, and the contract and all payment will be cancelled.

Yours etc.

Brian Chambers
Managing Director

What was that all about? And why did it feel as if ants were swarming in her stomach?

There was a beep outside the door. Connie shoved the letter and envelope back in the drawer and slammed it shut.

Dad came in. 'All sorted. I was right. P7 was just about to nose out of his cage.'

As he slipped the ID card into his trouser pocket, Connie glanced at the photo again. Maybe that was why it didn't look like him: he was using James Casey's room and had borrowed his card to get in. But why? Was he trying to impress her by pretending that he was the head of research, when really his job was more lowly?

'Ah.' Dad looked at the desk and tutted. 'I see Hue's made use of the facilities.' He took his diagram from the desk and slid the corner of the paper under the poop. A white blob slid on to the word

Hippocampus

Connie's eyes flicked to the letter on the armchair.

that moment when

Can blood actually freeze? Because it felt as if hers had stopped in her veins. Her mind, though, raced and swirled, hurling together three pieces of a jigsaw.

The photo on the card. The writing on the diagram. The name on the envelope. They couldn't fit together. They mustn't. Because if they did, the picture was too terrible to sit in her head.

But there it sat.

Keep breathing, she told herself, putting a hand to her heart to stop it jumping out. Her fingertips felt a bump beneath her T-shirt. Her locket.

'Dad,' she said in a friendly, faraway voice, 'I meant to tell you. Remember that locket of Mum's you gave me when I was tiny, with the picture of me as a baby? I've worn it all my life.'

He scrunched up the poop-speckled page. 'I'm so glad. She wore it all the time too, you know.' He turned and threw the paper into a bin by the desk.

'Except—' Connie's heart hammered like a policeman at the door. 'She didn't. Because I got it five months ago.' She pulled out the locket with trembling hands. 'From Ciara. For my birthday.' She popped it open to show the tiny photo of her and Ciara.

Dad turned round slowly. 'What?' He put a hand on the desk. 'Oh. Sorry, I thought you meant ...' He put his other hand to his head. 'I'm getting mixed up. It's all such a blur, love, I—'

'No, it's not. It's really clear.' Now her voice wasn't far away. It was loud and close and anything but friendly.

And before she realised that it might not be wise to say what she knew beyond doubt, the words tumbled out. 'You're not my dad!'

31. A Happy Lie or the Sad Truth?

They stared at each other for an endless moment. Connie's heart raced and froze, swelled and shrank, all at the same time.

Then Not-Dad did the last thing imaginable. He smiled. 'Guilty.' He raised his hands in surrender.

Her mouth fell open. A 'What?' fell out. Why wasn't he denying it, or at least looking shocked?

'I knew you'd find out sooner or later. The important thing is that you're here.' He paused. Panic exploded inside her. Here she was indeed, with this man – this un-Dad, this stranger. At night. And nobody knew where she was, except a boy across the sea.

'Don't be scared, Connie. This is what your dad would have wanted.' He held out a hand. 'James Casey.'

As if – as if – she'd shake it! 'I know. I mean I know

that's your name ... but who are you?' She wasn't making sense. But nor was anything else.

James Casey, Head of Research, perched his bottom on the desk. 'Your dad's best friend.'

'So where *is* my dad?' she said, in a voice as thin as frayed string.

'As I say, this is what he'd have wanted.' James stroked the desk and added softly, 'If he were still alive.'

Connie felt dizzy. The room swam around her. She sank into the armchair. It was too much. In one week her dad had gone from probably-not-alive, to definitely-in-front-of-her-alive, to now not in front of her *or* alive. She put her head in her hands and forced her breathing to slow. At last she looked up. 'What am I meant to believe?'

'That he loved you.'

She commanded the tears to stay behind her eyes. James Casey, Head of Research, mustn't see her cry. 'How dare you!' she said, channelling her fear into anger. 'Pretending to be my dad, playing with my memories – how did you know so much?' She glared into the eyes she'd thought she'd inherited. Amazing how the brown that had once seemed so warm and clear now looked muddy with deceit.

'He told me,' James said simply. 'When he'd recovered from the coma and lost you to Mags, he came back to Mexel Mann. He was even more determined to find a way to remove bad memories. We worked together on Mimi for five years. He really did recover, Connie. But it was a long time before he felt he could write you a proper letter.'

Connie forced a 'Why?' through the ice in her throat.

'Your dad wasn't ready to open up. He thought it could cause too much pain, for him and for you.'

She swallowed. Hadn't Mags said something similar? That the reason she'd hidden all his cards was to protect Connie from pain? *Oh, Mags. You were wrong – and right.* Wrong because withholding the cards and letter had caused its own pain; it had ruined Connie's chance of ever meeting her real dad. And right because if she'd never found that letter ... gone behind Mags's back ... emailed this man ... agreed to meet him ... come here ...

Connie pressed her knuckles into her knees. She should run. But where to? The door would only answer to the beep of James Casey's card.

'When you turned eleven,' James continued, 'your dad thought you were old enough for him to start explaining what had happened. And if you knew how sorry he was for leaving, it might begin the process of understanding and even forgiveness. But when you didn't answer his letter – well, he took it hard, got a bit desperate.' Despite smashing her trust into a million vicious pieces, he looked truly sad.

Connie felt the tears ramming the back of her eyes. *No!* She sniffed and said, as coldly and calmly as she could, 'What do you mean, "desperate"?'

James took off his glasses. At once Connie recognised the face from the ID card, now beardless and thinner. How could weight loss, a shave and a pair of glasses have fooled her so completely?

'Mimi was almost safe,' he said. 'Or so we thought. We'd tested dozens of chameleons successfully. It was time to move on to people. That's always a tricky stage in medical science.' He rested the glasses on his knee. 'As you pointed out, chameleon to human is a big leap. But over a year ago, after there was no reply to his letter, your dad was willing – determined, in fact – to take the risk.' James looked at Connie in a way she'd once have described as kind. 'He never got over losing you as well as your mum. He wanted to wipe the memory of the car crash, and the memory of leaving you at the airport. He said he had nothing to lose by trying out Mimi.'

'Except his whole life.' Now a disobedient tear did roll down Connie's cheek.

'He felt he'd already lost it,' James said softly. 'That it wasn't worth living with those memories. And even if Mimi didn't work for him – well, maybe one day she would, so that the shadow of what he'd done wouldn't hang over *your* life.'

'Mine? What's it got to do with ...?' Connie trailed off. A shapeless dread was spreading in her stomach. She looked at Hue, who was climbing down the leg of the desk in stripy blue and green ignorance. How lovely to have nothing to worry about except your next snack.

'Your dad,' said James, 'made me promise that, if he didn't make it, I'd keep working on Mimi. And when the procedure was safe and successful, I'd try and find you and tell you his story. He prepared for the worst: gave me access to his emails in case you ever got in touch, put his affairs in order. Just as well.' He looked down and fiddled with the glasses on his knee. 'There must have been some permanent damage from the pills he'd taken six years before, because his poor brain wasn't strong enough for Mimi.'

'How do you know?' Connie said fiercely. 'It could have been the other way round. Maybe it was the machine that was too strong – for anyone's brain.'

James smiled sympathetically. At least that's the word she would have used a couple of hours ago, but now she didn't trust herself to read his expression at all.

'Whatever the case, Mimi is now completely safe. After your dad ... well, I worked on Mimi, perfected her. And over the last year, she's proved a hundred per cent successful. Dozens of people have been through the procedure with no side effects at all.'

Connie blinked at him. 'Who?'

'So many. An old lady, for example, who remem-bered her cat falling into a lake when she was nine. She couldn't jump in to save it because she couldn't swim. She'd been haunted by that memory for seventy years.

And now ...' James flicked a hand, as if batting away a fly. 'Nothing. All she remembers is that she once had a cat and then she didn't. And the mind doesn't like gaps, Connie. It looks for stories to fill them. So I *reminded* –' he wiggled two fingers like speech marks – 'the old lady that her cat had run away from home. And that's what she now believes.'

'But it's not true.'

'Ex-soldiers,' he went on. 'Lots of them. Mimi erased their memories of shooting people, being shot at, grenades going off near them and other awful moments of war. All gone.' He spread out his hands. 'Better a happy lie than the sad truth, don't you think?'

'I ... I don't know.' Her mind was a fog. 'I mean, where do lies stop? You lied about being my dad. You could be lying about everything.'

James nodded slowly. 'I could. All I can say is, I'm not.' He turned his palms up, as if holding an invisible tray. 'I promise you, Connie, everything I told you about your dad – my best friend Ben – is true. The accident that killed your mum, his grief, the experiments and why he walked away at the airport. I pretended to be him because he *asked* me to, if you ever got in touch. He even gave me his passport. I couldn't believe it when your email arrived, a year and a half after he was ... unsuccessful with Mimi. Pretending to be him is my only lie, Connie – and I did it for him.'

'Why?' Connie stared at Hue, now picking his way across the carpet.

'So that you'd come here. That's what he wanted. You'd never have gone with a stranger. Even when you thought I was your dad, you were so brave to come with me.'

Brave? Connie cursed herself. *More like North-face-of-the-Eiger-without-a-rope stupid.* 'Why did he want me here?'

James Casey, Head of Research, slipped the glasses he didn't need into his pocket. 'Your dad said that when Mimi was ready and safe, he wanted you to use her to remove your memory of him. To free your life of that terrible sadness, to spare you what he went through.'

Connie clenched her fists in her lap. 'What if I don't *want* to remove his memory?'

James frowned. 'What? Why on earth wouldn't you?'

She couldn't explain the answer. But she could feel it. Leaning forward, she lifted Hue off the floor. She put him on her arm and rose from the chair.

'Mr Casey,' she said, as calmly as she could, 'please take us home.'

32. No Answer and the Only Answer

'I don't understand.' James stood up from the desk. 'Why not remove a memory that causes you nothing but pain?'

Connie went to the door. 'Please take us home,' she repeated.

He spread his arms, like the lead in a musical about to break into song. 'OK. Let me try again. Do you remember anything at all about your mum?'

Connie shook her head. Hue crept up her arm and sat on her shoulder.

'So, because you can't picture her smiling, or hear her singing you to sleep, does it hurt as much to think about her as it does about your dad?'

She said nothing. He knew the answer.

'I mean, you probably feel a vague sadness. But it's not personal, like your dad walking away. Hasn't that one tiny moment stained your whole life?'

Again, she didn't need to reply.

'Well, Mimi can remove that stain,' James said softly, 'by zapping the few memories you have of him, one by one. Starting with the café when you were four. Then the letter you found a week ago, then any other memories of him, however faint. That way your dad will become like your mum: nothing more than a fact, without a face or a voice.'

Zap ... nothing ... fact. The words rolled around Connie's head. She leaned against the door as a skinny tear ran down her cheek. He was right. The memory of Dad walking off *was* a burden, a stab of pain every time she recalled it. But there were other memories too: happy ones, if vague. Dad and her on the beach eating ice creams. Dad lifting her into his arms as they walked past a gate where a dog stood barking. Dad tucking her up in bed with a red duvet – or was it purple? It didn't matter; these were memories of love and safety and comfort that she'd have to lose along with the rest.

'Think how Mags would love it,' said James. 'She'd be the only parent you've ever known, no competition. Isn't that the best gift you could give her?'

Connie closed her eyes. Mags had taken her in, brought her up, loved her like a real daughter. But the memory of

Dad had stunted the love she'd felt able to return. Without it, she'd be free to love Mags as she deserved – like a parent. Again he was right. It would be the most wonderful gift.

'No memory, no pain. Come on, Connie.' An urgency crept into his voice. 'When it's gone, you won't miss it, like a hole that's been darned in a sock. Surely it's a no-brainer.'

Hole in a sock? No-brainer? Connie's eyes sprang open. How could he be so casual?

'If it's so easy, why don't *you* do it?' she said sharply. 'You must have some sad memory you could get rid of.'

'Please, Connie.' He clasped his hands together. 'Your dad wanted you to be free of him. I'm only trying to honour his wishes.'

'But what if they're not *my* wishes?' She hated the wobble in her voice.

He answered with his own question. 'Help me here. What do you gain by remembering?'

Hue shifted on her shoulder. She felt his little claws tickling her skin. 'My dad,' she said softly. Which was no answer and the only answer.

James gave her a long, deep look that bored through her eyes and right down to her toes. 'Is there nothing I can say to convince you?'

She shook her head, not trusting her voice.

He sighed. 'OK. I can see your mind's made up.' He stepped past her to the door. 'I'll take you to the airport hotel. You can stay there overnight and I'll put you on the plane tomorrow.' He beeped his card and opened the door.

She followed him down the corridor, her legs shaky with relief. Her right hand went to Hue on her left shoulder. She rested it on his back to steady him – or herself, she wasn't sure which.

'I'm sorry you feel this way,' said James, walking ahead. 'You must understand that your dad and I only wanted the best for you. And the results with others have been fantastic. I told you about the old lady and the soldiers. There's a teenage boy whose memory of an armed robbery has been wiped. He's no longer scared to be alone in his house. Civilians caught up in war – explosions, families killed, awfulness erased in a few painless minutes.'

'But I don't want my dad erased,' she said, feeling clearer with every step. 'Memories are all I have left of him.' She thought of Thyo and his diary collections. What was it he'd said? Something about memories being part of who he was. 'Maybe for some people it could be a wonderful thing – soldiers and the cat lady and the boy. But for me, losing Dad's memory would be losing part of me.'

She gave up trying to share the feelings that swirled inside her: the longing and loss and love for her dad; the strange peace of choosing the painful truth over a numbing lie, and the rush of love she felt for Mags who, she now realised, had done everything to protect her. Explaining all that would be like trying to fit Mount Everest into a matchbox.

James stopped at the door to the chameleon testing room. 'Ah.' He patted his pockets. 'I think I left my car keys in here. Just a sec.' He took out his card, beeped the door and opened it.

Suddenly, he grabbed Connie's arm. He bundled her into the room, followed her in and kicked the door shut behind them.

33. Bound

'What are you *doing*?' gasped Connie. 'Let me *go*!' Hue fell off her shoulder as James pulled her arms behind her back. She tried to jab him with her elbows. But they wiggled feebly, her wrists clamped in his grip. Hue scuttled across the floor and cowered in the corner, grey with terror.

'I gave you the chance to cooperate,' James snapped, hustling her towards the table in the middle of the room. 'But you're going to meet Mimi, whether you want to or not.' On the table lay lengths of rope. He must have prepared them when he'd come to 'close P7's cage'.

'You can't force me to do your experiment!' Connie kicked backwards against James's shin. He swore and stumbled, loosening his grip on her wrists. She broke free and rushed to the door. But without his card she'd never open it. 'Help!' she cried uselessly. She knew, somehow, that there was no-one beyond the door.

There was something beside it, though: the little red box of a fire alarm. And before James could grab her arms again, Connie pressed the glass.

'Damn you!' he hissed under the rising wail of the alarm. Dragging her across to the table, he pushed her into the chair. He brought her arms forward, held her wrists together with one hand and grabbed a rope with the other. Connie kicked his shin again. He swore, but this time his grip tightened. He came round the side, dodging her kicks, and tied her wrists to the left arm of the chair. Then he snatched another rope from the table and bent down. Grabbing her ankles, he tied them together. He looped the rope round the front right leg of the chair, again and again, before tying it in some intricate, invincible knot.

'Get *off* me!' she yelled.

James straightened up. 'Bloody alarm,' he muttered, glaring at her. 'I'll be back.' He rushed to the door and beeped his card. Then he was gone, the door shushing shut behind him.

Connie let out a roar. She wiggled her wrists but the rope held firm. She looked wildly round the room: at Hue, still trembling in the corner, and the cages round the wall. Every chameleon had dived for cover.

Mags had once told her how someone had prank-smashed a fire alarm in the Arrivals hall at the airport. The head cleaner had gone to turn it off at the main panel in the basement, but the fire services had come anyway, causing a right fuss. Connie prayed that James would have to go to the office basement *and* head off a fire engine or two, no doubt spinning some yarn about a faulty system or something. That would buy her some time.

For what? There was no way out.

Even if she could escape the ropes, the only exit apart from the door was the window James had talked about, at the top of the far wall above a cage. At least *that* fact was true. As for everything else he'd told her, how could she know what to believe?

'You lying monster!' she shouted over the whine of the alarm. Then, 'You idiot!' she shouted at herself. There had been clues all along that he wasn't her dad. Now they stung like wasps. The marshmallow worms: when her real dad had told James about leaving little Connie at the café, he must have skipped the part where she'd spat them out; her real dad wouldn't have got that wrong. The photos of her mum: James had said that they were tucked away in his attic, conveniently unavailable. And Mags rushing up in Terminal 2 and not recognising 'Dad' at first – because she didn't! James had clearly made some changes to resemble her dad – wearing the glasses, shaving his beard – and had used lies and the power of suggestion for the rest. What was it he'd said? Something about his hair being thinner because he was older? When really it was because he wasn't *Dad*! And Mags had sensed that, until he'd smooth-talked her out of it.

Mags, whom she'd hated for hiding her dad's cards. Mags, whose white lies, out of love and concern, now paled against the massive deceit of James Casey.

'I'm so sorry, Mags!' Connie burst out. Leaning down to the left, she tried to bite at the rope round her wrists. But her clumsy teeth merely bruised the skin and damp-ened the rope so that it sank further in. She put her head on her arm and gave a kind of roaring sob.

There was a rustle from the cage on her left. She looked up. Peter's little head poked out between the leaves. He moved slowly along a branch, stopped and fixed Connie with busy, bright eyes. In the next cage along, another chameleon – V6 it said on the sign – peeked out from the undergrowth.

Connie sat up. 'I'm as trapped as you are.' She shook her head furiously. James was using her, just like the chameleons, as a pawn in his experiments. 'Who's the real cold-blooded one?!' she shouted.

Hue was creeping towards her. A faint green trickled into his back. His legs were hinting at pink.

She stared at the door. The alarm wailed on. She pictured James reaching the basement, turning off the sound, waiting for the fire brigade, heading them off with some story and then returning. To do what? Wipe her memory with that machine? But why, against her will, when dozens of volunteers had already proved it was safe?

Volunteers. Connie caught her breath. That letter in James's drawer ... hadn't it said something about volunteers? Something about safety – or rather *proving* it.

And in an instant she knew. There *were* no volunteers. The old lady, the soldiers, the boy: James had made them all up, along with so much else. *She* was his human guinea pig! She gave a whimper of terror.

Hue reached her chair. He put one front foot on her left trainer, then the other. His tiny two-pronged hands clasped her laces.

'Untying my shoe won't help,' she muttered. He shot her a haughty, don't-rush-me look. He lifted his front right foot and grasped the side of her ankle. His left foot gripped the other side, and now he was climbing her trouser leg with slow, methodical steps.

'What's your plan?' she said – because he definitely had one. Over her knee he clambered, along to her hip and up on to the left arm of the chair. He perched on her forearm.

'You're tickling me!' She tried to wriggle her arm but the ropes held it firm. 'And I can't scra– *aah*.' His head shot down to her wrist. 'Wow! Hue, you're amaz–*aah*.' He'd seen her efforts to bite the ropes and he was copying what she'd done! The difference was that his teeth were smaller and his claws sharper. In his lizardy way, he understood enough to know that she was trapped. She'd have hugged him if she could. 'Go, Huey!' she breathed.

The alarm was still blaring. Never had such a plaintive, persistent sound been so welcome. The longer it lasted, the more time she had. 'That's it, yes, brilliant.' Hue nibbled away. 'Ow!' He nipped her skin as his teeth missed the rope. 'It's OK, keep it up, you can do it, go on, Huey.' Nibble, nip. She twisted her wrists. Nibble, nip, again and again, and—

'You did it!' Her hands flew forward. Hue crept on to her arm. And never mind his snooty look that seemed to say, 'You didn't actually *doubt* me, did you?' – she planted a kiss on his scaly head.

34. Uncaged

Connie bent forward to untie the rope that bound her ankles to the chair leg. It was super-tight. Trust James Casey, Head of Research, to know all the best knots.

'Help me, Hue, quick.'

While he crawled down her leg to gnaw at the ankle rope, Connie unzipped the pocket of her hoodie, still tied around her waist. Thank goodness for the phone James didn't know she had. No wonder he'd refused to buy her one: so that she couldn't contact anyone. That story about researching brain damage from phone waves was no doubt another lie. Well, thank goodness she'd kept her stupidphone secret, albeit for different reasons.

As she took it from her pocket, the alarm stopped. *Oh no.* James must have disabled it in the basement. Once the fire brigade came – *if* they came – it wouldn't take long for him to charm them away and then come back upstairs.

With shaking fingers, Connie pressed Thyo's number. 'Answer me,' she begged. On the fourth ring, she whisper-yelled, 'Thyo!' as if her voice would burst out of his phone.

And maybe it did, because at last he replied. 'Hey, Connie, how's it go—?'

'I've been tied up. Kidnapped!'

'*What?*' She could almost hear the words crashing through his skull. 'Where are you? Where's your dad?'

'He's not my dad. Can't explain. Phone the Leeds police. Get them to come to Mexel Mann. I'm on the fourth floor, in the testing room.'

'What do you mean he's not your ... what's going *on?*'

'Just phone the police!' Connie ended the call.

She looked down. 'Well done, Huey.' He'd bitten through the rope. She wriggled her leg free. Scooping him up, she ran over to the cage beneath the little window.

She slipped him into the pouch still round her neck. Then she gripped the mesh of the cage and raised a foot to climb. Hue squirmed on her chest. 'Keep still!'

she muttered. But he twisted away, dived out from her hoodie and scurried across the mesh to the cage door. Using his mouth and a pincer hand, he pulled at the bolt. It didn't move.

'What are you doing? We have to go.' Connie reached out to collect him. He dodged her grasp, climbed down to the floor and darted along to the next cage. 'Come back, Hue!'

He was climbing the mesh. Inside, P8 crept forward along a branch. Hue began to worry the bolt of the cage door with his mouth.

Connie gasped. This selfish recluse, who hated other chameleons, was trying to free them! 'We haven't got time, Huey.'

But while her mouth spoke what was true, her legs did what was right. She ran to each cage, pulling the bolts and opening the doors. One by one, nervous heads poked out between leaves. Then nervous bodies and, finally, long, confident tails that seemed to lead from behind, pushing the creatures out of their cages and down to the floor.

'That's it, guys,' Connie said. 'Come with me.' And whether they understood her speech or her action, the chameleon crowd – two words that simply shouldn't go together – followed her across the room.

As she reached the cage by the window, her phone rang.

'The police wouldn't listen,' came Thyo's frantic voice. 'They thought it was a prank call. Connie, what's going on?'

'Keep trying. Don't stop till they come. And don't call again. I've escaped from the ropes – I'll phone you when I can.' She turned off her phone and zipped it up in her hoodie pocket. James could be back any second; if it rang, or even buzzed on silent, it might give her away. She raised her right foot and tried to wedge it in the mesh of the cage. But the tip of her trainer was too wide. She'd do better without shoes. *Especially ones bought by James Casey.*

There was a beep. Before Connie could pull off her trainers, the door began to open. Her mind went blank. But her body thought for her. She dived round the side of the cage and crouched by the wall as James came in, pushing something. It was a pole on wheels with a dome on top, like one of those driers Mags sat under at the hairdresser, or a giant – *desk lamp.* Connie's heart rammed her ribs like a shark against a boat. Of course. A human-sized memory wiper.

'What the—?' James took in the empty chair, the ropes on the ground, the chameleons on the floor – and Connie.

She sprang to her feet, reached up and clutched the mesh of the cage. But again her trainer wouldn't wedge between the wires.

James raced over. He grabbed her arms and yanked them behind her. 'Remember,' he snapped, dragging her towards the machine, 'your dad. The airport. The café.' He was bringing the memory to the front of her mind, ready to be zapped.

'No!' she yelled. But the more desperately she tried not to think of it, the more brightly it blazed in her mind.

James pushed her under the machine. He released a catch on the pole and pushed the dome down until it fitted her head like a hat. Then he crouched down to turn on a switch at the base ...

And yelled. A chameleon was biting his finger. He tried to shake it off but its jaws were clamped. Connie ducked and dived out from the dome.

'Aah!' James roared, as another chameleon bit his ankle. A third crawled on to his shoe. 'Get off!' He shook his foot. But as the creature fell off, a fourth chameleon shot up his other leg and under his jacket. 'Yoww!' He snatched it away. Another one ran up his arm and clutched his chest like a vicious living brooch. One reached his head and tore at his hair; yet another one clung to his face. For every creature he pulled off, another took its place. Chameleons piled on top of him in a clamber-fest of gouging and biting.

As James twisted away to fight them off, Connie darted behind him to the cage beneath the window. She pulled off her trainers and threw them through the open cage door into the dense foliage. Hiding her shoes might buy her a few precious seconds before James worked out that she'd removed them to climb the cage and out of the window. And now she scaled the mesh easily, nimble and silent in her socked feet. At the top, she crept across the roof of the cage to the window.

Suddenly, below her, the chameleons looked up. Like a many-headed creature, they turned together from their prey. They flowed across the floor towards the cage and Connie, leaving behind them the scratched and bitten heap of human misery that was James Casey, Head of Research.

35. Don't Look Down

On top of the cage, Connie stood at the window. The bottom of the frame was level with her waist. She twisted the handle and pushed the window out. Chameleons surged up the cage behind her. They could easily wriggle past and through the gap. But they held back, as if refusing to escape before her. Only one moved through the crowd towards her. Hue crept on to her hand, then darted up her arm and on to the window frame. He slipped through the gap and dropped on to a ledge outside. Turning to face her, he cocked his head, as if to say, 'Easy peasy, follow me.'

It was a narrow ledge.

'Don't even think about it!' came James's voice. She looked back down into the room. He was staggering to his feet. 'We're four floors up!'

She turned to the window and leaned out. Night air smacked up her nostrils, smoky and thick with cold. *Don't look down.*

She looked down.

Streetlights bathed the road in a buttery fuzz. The buildings opposite glowed dimly. A car passed, its faint growl reminding her that she must be fifteen, maybe twenty, metres above the ground.

'Connie, stop!' James shouted. Glancing back, she saw him standing at the bottom of the cage, ramming a pointy shoe into the mesh. He'd worked out her escape route already.

She pressed her palms on the window frame and pushed her whole body through. Twisting side-ways, she lay face-down along the window ledge. She clutched the frame with her left hand and drew her knees forward. Then she pulled herself up and sat on her heels, so that she was kneeling on the ledge. Hue crept on to her shoulder. The other chameleons stayed inside. From their hissing, and James's swear-ing, she guessed they must be attacking him as he climbed the cage.

Connie took in her surroundings. To the left of the ledge was a stretch of smooth metal wall, then another ledge. Beyond that, the Mexel Mann tower ended and the next building began. It was lower and had a flat roof. There was a pipe running vertically upwards where the two buildings joined. If only she could get to that pipe, she could shin up to the flat roof. But the next ledge was about three metres away, and there was that gap of sheer wall in between. It was too far even for her to—

'*Aaah!*' she cried.

James's fingers closed round the wrist of her left hand, which was still clasping the window frame. With his other arm he fought off chameleons. 'You're safe now. Come in.'

'Never! I'm safer out here.' She tried to pull her hand away, but his grip was solid.

'Think, Connie. What's worse to lose: your memory or your life? *Ow*, get *off* me!' He pulled a chameleon off his chest and hurled the creature away across the top of the cage. 'If you want to honour your dad's life, don't waste yours. He died to help you and others.'

Connie looked out across the city, a Legoland of rooftops and towers glowing under the star-spattered sky. 'I know I'm your test case. I know you made up all those volunteers. You couldn't *get* any volunteers because no-one would risk their life on that machine. And if you don't, that Medi-thing company won't pay you.' She twisted her wrist.

James squeezed harder. 'You need to finish your dad's work. Can't you see what good it could do, to free people of bad memories?'

A cold clarity pierced Connie's terror. 'Only if they choose it. What if they don't want to be freed? What if it's not freedom at all? What if taking their memories takes their personality too? What if the machine's used to control people, to dupe them? What if it gets into the wrong hands? Like *yours*!' She tugged until her arm felt as though it would burst from her shoulder socket. 'Let me GO!'

'You stubborn, selfish ...' James yanked her wrist towards him. She jerked sideways, her left ear slamming against the bottom of the open window. Tears of pain leaked down her cheeks. Hue clung to her right shoulder.

With one hand still clamping her wrist, James shot his other arm through the window. He grabbed her waist and pulled. Hue darted down from her shoulder and bit his finger.

'*Aaah!*' James gasped. Connie felt his grip on her left wrist weaken. She wrenched her hand free. In the rebound, she teetered to the right. The street swam below her. She grasped the edge of the ledge to steady herself. *Don't look down.* Hue scampered off her lap and up the side of the window to the top of the frame. On her left, James reached for her again. Praying that the chameleons inside would find another way to escape him, Connie slammed the window down on his arm. He yelped in pain and pulled it inside. She closed the window completely. Better to sit it out here than to go back inside to that machine, even though she'd just shut off her only escape route from the ledge.

Almost. As Connie stretched her arm up to rescue Hue, it was Hue who rescued her.

Don't look down. Look up.

Above the window, between this ledge and the next one, a huge glowing S stuck out from the wall on steel rods: the last letter in the name across the building.

Mexel Mann Solutions really was her solution.

36. The Letter and the Law

Hue was the first to go. He perched at the top of the window and looked up at the S, as if working out his route. Turning his back to the giant letter, he stretched up his long tail and curled it round the lowest of the rods joining the S to the wall. He walked upside down, climbing the wall with his tail wrapped round the rod. Then he twisted his body upright and perched on the rod.

My arms are as good as his tail, Connie told herself, and tried to believe it. She reached up and hooked her fingers round the bottom curve of the S. Then she pulled herself up, walking up the wall. The metal pressed an aching cold through her socks and into her feet. She heaved her body forward over the base of the S and hung from her waist with her legs and arms dangling, draped like a towel over a washing line.

'Where are you?' came James's panicky voice. She heard the window creak open again. She hoisted her legs up and turned sideways so that she was kneeling in the cradle of the S. She crouched on all fours, small and silent, begging the darkness to hide her.

'Connie?' James called. She didn't dare peep over, but guessed he was leaning out of the window looking down. There was real fear in his voice.

'Thank God,' she heard him mutter, presumably on seeing that she hadn't fallen. 'So where have you ...?' There was a pause. She imagined him looking up. 'Connie?' She shrank in her metal hammock. 'You're inside that S, aren't you?'

'Hello?' A woman's voice called from far below. There was the sound of a car door slamming. 'What's going on up there?

'I, ah – hello, officer,' James shouted down.

'We had a call to come and investigate this building,' called the woman. 'Several, actually. From a boy, then his mother. Something about a *kidnap*.'

Naledi! thought Connie. The police hadn't listened to Thyo so he'd told his ma. And of course they'd had to follow up. Who could ignore that sure, sunshine voice? Connie mind-hugged her.

'So if you'd please let us in.'

'Um – yes, of course. Coming.'

There was silence. Connie had to act fast. James would think up some story for the police and send them away again. Then he'd head up to the fifth floor. The window ledge was above the S and he'd climb down to get her.

Connie looked up at Hue, still clinging to the rod of the S. 'Come on,' she murmured, holding out her palm. He manoeuvred himself across from the rod and down on to her shoulder. She hugged her arms round the bottom of the S and lowered her right leg. Her toes searched the wall but couldn't feel the next ledge. She pointed her socked foot. Nothing. She was stuck on the S with nowhere to go.

Hue crept from her shoulder and down her back. What was he doing? On he crawled, down her right leg to her foot. She felt him perch there for a second. Then he was gone.

Had he found the ledge and jumped down to it? She couldn't look round; she'd lose her grip. Or had he tried and missed? That was unthinkable. And the ache in her arms was unbearable. She had to hold on. She couldn't hold on. Her arms were breaking, she was losing her grip.

Something tickled her right foot. It brushed her big toe, nudged it up a bit, right a bit, down a bit and – 'Ohhh,' she breathed as her toes found the ledge. Her heel descended, her other leg dropped, her hands let go – and now she was crouching on the ledge. A tear of relief ran down her cheek.

'Thanks, Huey.' She stroked the tail that had guided her to safety.

It paused for a second. Then Hue was off again. Connie followed him to the end of the ledge. She watched as he grasped the pipe and scurried up the couple of metres to the flat roof of the neighbouring building. He stopped at the top and turned his head.

Connie took a deep breath. A simple pipe. So what if it was at least fifteen metres above the ground? So what if it was dark and a wind was beginning to snatch at her hair?

'Muchu Chhish,' she whispered. 'I can do this.'

She reached up her arms. Her fingers found – *yes!* – a ridge. It must be a bracket attaching the pipe to the wall.

She grasped it and pulled herself up, breathing in the sour paint-and-metal smell. She frog-bent her legs out, reached up again. Grasp, pull and bend ... and again. With a final effort, she heaved herself on to the flat roof. She lay on her front, her arms either side, her chin resting on the freezing, glorious grit.

'We did it, Hue!' His outline trembled in front of her. She felt rather than saw his colour in the darkness: dull with exhaustion and cold. Sitting up, she lifted him gently into the pouch on her front. Then she untied her hoodie from her waist and put it on, easing it carefully over him.

From below came the sound of a car door slamming. Connie spun on her bottom and shuffled to the edge of the roof. She huddled against the side wall of Mexel Mann and peered down, just in time to see the police car drive off.

James would be on his way up to the fifth floor now. Connie wished she could see his face when he looked down on the empty S. But however smart she'd been to escape, he was smarter. It wouldn't be hard for him to work out her route and find another way up here. Holding her hand to her chest to protect Hue, she stood up and ran across the roof.

37. Socks on the Streets

Every footstep stung as Connie raced across the gravel on the flat roof. But she was grateful for the stones that bit through her socks, keeping her focused and alert.

She stopped abruptly. The roof ended just in front of her. Standing on the edge, she looked down on to a narrow street. There were a few parked cars but no people about. Good – James hadn't figured out her route and come to meet her at the bottom. And bad – if he *did* suddenly appear, there was no-one to help her.

A couple of metres below her on the left, a tiled roof slanted steeply over the street. Beneath that was a lamp post. Connie turned. Holding on to the edge of the flat roof, she lowered her legs down the wall of the building. She hung there for a second then let go. Pain jarred up her legs as she landed on the sloping roof below. She dropped to her knees. Leaning forward, she rested for a moment with her forehead on the tiles to calm her galloping heart. Then she crawled down the roof, careful to give Hue space in his pouch.

At the base of the roof she turned round and sat with her legs dangling over the gutter. The top of the lamp post was a metre below. There was a tiny crossbar under the lamp. 'We can do this, Huey,' she murmured. 'We have to.' But 'have to' and 'can' were very different things.

Connie stretched her legs out until her feet felt the crossbar. Twisting to the left, she reached out her right arm, leaned across the space and – *yes!* – grasped the post beneath the lamp with her right hand. She kind of sprang, kind of lurched across until she was half-sliding, half-falling down the pole.

Oh, the relief of solid ground! She leaned against the lamp post. But there was no time to rest. James could be searching the streets right now. She had to get – where? Well, home, obviously, which meant the airport. But how to get *there* wasn't obvious at all.

Connie ran to the end of the street, a T junction that joined a main road. Even at this time of night it was busy with cars and pedestrians. A taxi, maybe? *Money!* With a jolt she remembered the change that James had let her keep after buying her trainers. From the front pocket of her jeans she pulled out the five-pound note and two-pound coin.

For once she welcomed the crowd milling along the pavement: gaggles of nightclubbers, couples arm in arm. For once they offered protection, not threat. If James appeared, she could dodge between bodies, slip down side streets, hide like Hue amid the leaves of his cage. But unlike him, her camouflage lay in movement, merging with the flow of people. *And please, no-one look down.* Her socked feet stuck out like, well – sore thumbs.

A taxi approached along the road. She held out her arm like they did in films.

The car drew up and the driver leaned across the passenger seat. 'Where to, love?' He had a friendly, concerned, grandad-of-the-year kind of face. At any other time that would be lovely but, right now, his friendly concern might lead to questions – the last thing Connie needed.

'The airport, please,' she said, trying to fake the confidence of Thyo and the coolness of Abri.

And failing. "Ow old are you, love?' The driver frowned. 'Where's your mum and dad?'

'They're, um, waiting for me at the airport. I ... got left behind.' *How lame is that?* Cursing herself, Connie continued, 'They told me to get a taxi.'

'They did?' The driver made a face like Mrs Farrell's when Billy Kerr once said he'd left his homework on the ceiling. But as another taxi drew up behind, the driver said, 'OK, then. 'Op in.'

'How much will it be?'

'Depends on traffic. Around thirty quid.'

'Oh.' Connie's fist clenched round her money. 'I've only got ...' *Don't tell him. He's suspicious enough.* 'It's OK, actually. Thanks.' She shrank back.

'Oy,' said the driver. 'What's going on?'

Connie turned from the car and fled along the pavement. She wove between the pedestrians, stubbing her toes on wonky paving stones and nearly bumping into a woman standing at a bus stop.

'Sorry,' Connie gasped, and, *Of course*, she thought. 'Excuse me, do you, um, is there a bus to the airport from here?'

The woman looked up. 'The Flyer. City Square.'

'Where's that?'

The woman pointed down the road. 'First bus stop on the right.'

'Thanks,' Connie breathed, and ran on before the woman could ask any awkward questions. Her feet were freezing. Every step jarred up her legs.

Reaching the bus stop, she went inside the shelter and sat cross-legged on the bench. She tucked her feet beneath her thighs to warm them up and hide them from passers-by, praying that a bus would appear before James did, and that she could bluff her way through.

Ten minutes later a blue and orange bus drew up with 'Flyer' written along the side. Two people got out.

Connie climbed on to the bus. The driver, a young man with a bored, pointy face, was staring ahead and drumming his hands on the wheel. Thank goodness he didn't see her feet.

'Single to the airport, please,' she said, not daring to say 'child' and desperately hoping she had enough for an adult ticket. Just as she was steeling herself to explain that her parents had gone ahead, and her gran had dropped her at the bus stop, and, and, and ... the driver said, without even looking at her, 'Three fifty.'

Connie hugged him with her heart and pushed the five-pound note towards him. She took the change and scurried past the other passengers: a man wearing headphones and an elderly couple with their eyes closed.

She sat at the back of the bus. As it growled out of Leeds, she dared to relax. Relief poured its syrup inside her. After all her running, now the bus was running for her, shedding the city, the day and James Casey like a wicked skin.

Connie leaned back. She should phone Thyo, let him know she was OK and thank him for getting Naledi to call the police.

Naledi. The name lodged like lead in her brain. She unzipped her hoodie pocket. Taking her phone out, she turned it on and pressed Thyo's number.

He answered after one ring. 'Connie! I've been phoning you all—'

'Your ma. I know you had to tell her, but I bet she'll try and contact Mags through the airport. You've got to stop her. Mags mustn't know any of this.'

'Mags won't know a thing, because Ma doesn't either. I got Abri to impersonate her.'

'What?' The words danced through Connie. 'Thyo, you're amazing.'

'Are you OK, Connie? Tell me what's happening!'

'I'm fine now.' She stared through the window at the gleam and blur of night. Exhaustion swept through her. 'Long story. I'll tell you when I get back tomorrow.'

'Where *are* you?'

'On my way to the airport.'

'*What?* It's nearly midnight! Where will you sleep?'

'In the airport. I'm grand, really. Talk tomorrow.' She pressed END CALL and turned off her phone. Right now, she couldn't face Thyo's questions or a lecture, starting with 'I *told* you not to go'.

Closing her eyes, Connie let her limbs melt into the bristly seat like butter into toast. All she had to do was wait at the airport until the flight tomorrow morning. *The flight!* Her eyes sprang open. Her hand flew to her hoodie pocket and – 'Ohhh,' she breathed, feeling the sharp edge of her passport. Thank goodness she'd kept it on her. She brought it out, dizzy at the thought of how scuppered she'd have been without it.

Her hand froze. How scuppered she *was*. Because never mind her passport – her ticket back to Dublin was with James.

38. Meena the Cleaner

Connie stepped off the bus. On the positive side, she told herself, James would be less likely to come looking for her at the airport if he knew she couldn't get home.

On the negative side – well, she couldn't get home.

Trying to swallow her panic, she went through the sliding doors of the airport. She blinked in the bright, horribly cheerful light of the entrance area and ran through her options. It didn't take long because there was only one: to phone Thyo. He'd have to spill the beans to Ned or Naledi so that they could book her a ticket home in time for Mags to suspect nothing. The details were sketchy; how would they get the ticket to Connie? What if they flipped and told Mags? But there was no other choice. Still holding her passport in her right hand – she hadn't dared to let go of it – Connie's left hand went to her hoodie pocket.

And stopped. A bomb exploded in her chest.

The zip was open. Her pocket was flat. Her phone had gone.

She looked at the ground. She spun round. She ran back through the entrance doors and retraced her steps to the bus stop. No phone.

Walking back into the airport Connie replaced her passport in her hoodie pocket and made quadruple sure she zipped it up. A stillness settled over her panic, like ice over a rushing river. She felt strangely unconcerned, as if all her worry, shock and fear had been used up for the day, leaving behind a dull, clinical logic as cold as the concrete through her socks. She must have forgotten to zip up her pocket after taking out her passport. Her phone must be on the bus which, right now, was speeding back to Leeds. She had no way to contact Thyo, no ticket, no shoes, no ideas. She was stuck.

'Oh dear,' she said, as if she'd chipped a fingernail or seen a small rain cloud. 'What now, Hue?' She pulled out the neck of her hoodie and looked down. His poor little head was dull brown with dehydration. At least she could get him some water. Not from the bathroom; tap water might upset his delicate stomach.

The WH Smith on the left was closed. But beside it was a vending machine. Connie scurried across the gleaming floor tiles, hoping nobody would notice her shoeless feet. Not that there *was* anybody much at this hour: just a couple walking off towards a sign on the right that said 'International Arrivals' and a cleaner pushing her trolley. *Mags*, thought Connie. A needle pierced her numbness at this reminder of the person she suddenly missed more than anyone in the world.

At the vending machine she used her remaining money to buy a Crunchie bar and a bottle of water. If only vending machines sold crickets!

Finishing the Crunchie in three bites, Connie stuffed the wrapper in her pocket and went into the ladies' toilet to the right of the machine. She sat in a cubicle and pulled out the nozzle of the water bottle. Then she held out the neck of her hoodie with one hand and dripped water into Hue's mouth. 'There you go,' she murmured as his brown head trickled back to blue.

Connie came out of the cubicle. Standing at the sink, she thought of the toilets in Dublin airport and the Miles family coming in to wash. What would Thyo be doing now? Probably sleeping soundly, now that she'd told him she was fine and would be back tomorrow. She leaned forward, pressed her forehead against the mirror and moaned.

'You all right, love?' said a voice.

She jerked her head up and stared in the mirror. The cleaner stood behind, with one hand on her trolley.

'I, um.' Connie turned round.

'Where are your shoes?' The ID card pinned to her T-shirt said her name was Meena Khan.

Connie opened her mouth. But every excuse and explanation, fib and fabrication, dissolved on her tongue as she stared at Meena Khan.

'You on your tod?' Meena's eyes were kind and brown.

Connie had had enough of kind brown eyes. She turned to go.

'You must be with *someone*. It's midnight. Do you know where they went? I'll go and find 'em, shall I?'

But suddenly, Connie didn't want her to go anywhere. Meena Khan looked nothing like Mags; she was small and slight and her hair was black and straight, not browny-grey and curly. But her voice was warm and her name began with M and she smelt very faintly of lemon cleaning spray. Connie felt her chin wobble. 'I need to get home. To Ireland. I lost my ticket.'

Meena frowned. 'And that's why you've got no shoes? And why you're alone here at midnight?'

Connie blinked.

'It's OK, love. I'm staff. I can help.'

Connie sniffed.

'How about a comfy seat and a cup of hot chocolate, and you can tell me what's going on?'

Connie didn't know if it was the hand on her arm, or the gentle voice, or the mention of hot chocolate that made her burst into tears.

Pushing the trolley, Meena led Connie out of the ladies across the entrance hall to the empty check-in area. There was a row of seats in the corner. 'Sit down there.' She took a tissue from her pocket and held it out. 'Now, what's this all about?'

'Thanks.' Connie pressed the tissue into her eyes. 'There's this man, James Casey. He was chasing me. He's got a machine. He tied me up.' It was coming out all wrong but she couldn't stop. 'I escaped through a window ... the chameleons helped me ... I was four floors up.' She was gabbling now. 'I climbed up a pipe ... down a lamp post ... I got the bus ... lost my pho-o-*ohh*.' More tears tumbled out.

'It's OK, love.' Astonishment danced in Meena's eyes, and questions twitched on her lips, but she held them in. 'Take your time. When you're ready, let's try again.'

Connie felt Hue wriggle in in his pouch. She drew deep, slow breaths to settle him. If anyone here found out she had a chameleon on her chest, they might not let him fly home with her – however and whenever that would be. As he calmed, she relaxed too. She recounted the events of the evening again, as clearly as she could, without mentioning Hue. She'd got as far as sliding down the lamp post when Meena grasped her hand and said firmly, 'OK, love. We're going to security.'

39. Shoes to the Rescue

An hour later Connie was telling her story for the third time. She'd given a potted version to the man in security, who'd phoned the police. Now Sergeant Firth from Leeds Central Police Station was sitting opposite her in a café beside the International Arrivals area. He had a bald head and fearsome eyebrows that rose like fighting bears as she explained how James had pretended to be her long-lost dad, lured her to Leeds and tied her up to test an unsafe memory-wiping machine. She kept it as simple as possible; it sounded crazy enough, and so much of what James had told her might be lies.

When she'd finished, Sergeant Firth stared at his notepad.

'You do believe me, don't you?' she said at last.

He looked up. Beneath those ferocious brows, his eyes were warm. 'I want to say yes, love, but ...' He tapped the notepad with a pen. 'When airport security phoned us, we sent two officers to Mexel Mann to investigate.' He looked at his watch. 'That was about three-quarters of an hour ago, at eleven thirty. They'd already gone there earlier, at about nine thirty, after a series of phone calls.' He glanced at his notebook. 'They spoke to James Casey, then left Mexel Mann at about nine forty-five.'

'I know,' said Connie. 'I was on the roof. I saw them drive off. Those calls were from my friend's sist— mum.'

'Well, Mr Casey told the officers they were from animal rights nutters trying to get him into trouble for perfectly legal animal testing.'

Connie drew a sharp breath. Was there no end to that man's deceit?

'What I'm saying,' said Sergeant Firth, 'is that James Casey had from nine forty-five until eleven thirty before the officers came back. Don't you think that if he'd tied you up, and you'd escaped, he'd assume you'd go to the police? Surely he'd use that time to get away.'

Connie stared at the sergeant. 'Didn't he?'

'Quite the opposite. On my way here, I got a call from the officers to say that James had answered the door and let them into Mexel Mann. He'd willingly taken them up to the testing lab on the fourth floor. They'd just gone in when they called me. Said there was no sign of any trouble.'

'What?!' Connie gasped. 'That's impossible.' But as she said it, she thought of that hour and three-quarters between the police visits. Instead of searching for her, meticulous James Casey could have returned the chameleons to their cages, tidied up and changed his shirt, even put new glass in the fire alarm. He could have mopped and wiped away blood, fingerprints and all evidence of their fight. Then, with his smooth-talking confidence, he could easily cook up some story.

Which, of course, he had. Sergeant Firth put down his pen and said, 'When the officers asked about you, James said, sure, you'd been there. He told them you begged him to bring you to Leeds in the first place, and that you wanted to see his work. But while he was showing you round Mexel Mann, you got upset about the chameleon testing. He saw you run off down a corridor. He went after you, but you gave him the slip in that maze of a building. He was looking for you, and was just about to phone the police, when they turned up anyway.'

Connie shook her head. It was so ridiculous, so outrageous, so ... James. He'd joined the few dots of fact with twisted lines to create his own false picture of events. 'I promise you,' she said, tears pricking her eyes, 'he tied me up, tried to force me under that machine. There was a fight.'

The fight!

'What about the scratches?' she said. 'On his face and neck and hands, from the chameleons?'

'He told the officers he gets those all the time doing his tests; those chameleons have sharp claws and teeth.'

She flicked away a furious tear. 'I'm telling the truth! You've *got* to believe me.'

Sergeant Firth gave what Connie hoped was a sympathetic look; it was hard to tell under those eyebrows. At last he said gently, 'You know what? I do believe you. But without more evidence, it could end up as your word against his.'

'He pretended to be my dad! Even if I couldn't prove anything else, surely that's a crime?'

He sighed. 'Not necessarily, I'm afraid: only if it's done to commit an offence. And from what you've told me,

James could claim he did it for good reasons, to fulfil your dad's wishes. If there was something else to prove he's lying, that would really help us.'

Connie laced her fingers in her lap. *If only Hue could talk.* He'd seen it all. The other chameleons, too, were her witnesses, silent and stuck back in their cages.

Their cages. Her heart gave a lurch. *Of course!* 'Are those two officers still at Mexel Mann?' she said quickly.

'Probably. Either still questioning James or looking round the lab.'

'Can you get them to ask him what shoes I was wearing when he saw me run off? And to record his answer.' She couldn't get the words out fast enough. 'Then go to the cage below the window and look in the undergrowth. My shoes are there – blue Nike trainers.' She moved her chair out from the table and wiggled her socked feet. 'I took them off and threw them in before I climbed the cage. That'll prove he's lying about seeing me run down a corridor in my shoes.'

Sergeant Firth smacked the table, grinning. As he stood up and took his walkie talkie from his belt, Connie prayed that James had been too busy fighting off chameleons to see her escape in her socks.

The sergeant paced up and down the Arrivals hall, talking, waiting for the reply, talking and waiting. While his back was turned, Connie put her hand to her chest. 'Well done, Huey,' she whispered. He hadn't wriggled once during the interview, as if sensing the need to stay hidden.

Ten minutes later the sergeant returned. 'Bingo!' Even his eyebrows seemed to beam. 'James Casey told Constable Dyer that you were wearing some blue Nike trainers when you ran off down the corridor. He said he remembers them well because he bought them for you himself. Then Constable Peters found them in the cage! So it would seem that our Mr Casey *didn't* see you running down the corridor in shoes – or, I'd suggest, at all.' The sergeant winked. 'He's on his way to the station right now, in the capable hands of our constables.'

He sat down at the table. 'Oh, and I just had a message to say your friend's mum phoned the station again. They told her you're safe and sound with me and we'll sort you out a ticket for tomorrow morning.' He leaned across the table and gave her a fond-but-stern-uncle kind of look. 'Talking of mums, we need to phone yours.'

Connie's triumph evaporated. 'Oh,' she said faintly, not bothering to correct 'mum' to 'foster mum'. She was too busy picturing Mags's incredulous, speechless, beyond-furious face as she picked up the phone at half past midnight to a policeman in Leeds. Options raced through her mind. She could say, 'I've forgotten Mags's number.' She could say, 'She lost her phone – she hasn't got a phone – she doesn't speak English – she doesn't *speak*.'

But she didn't. Because, as the excuses got wilder, they seemed to fill up with air and float right out of her head, leaving behind a calm, clear resolution. *No more lies.*

40. Sorries and Stories

After speaking to Mags, Sergeant Firth passed the phone to Connie. Her hand shook as she held it to her ear.

'Hello?'

'Connie?' came Mags's tiny voice. And that was enough to get Connie crying, which was enough to get Mags crying, which meant they didn't say much at all beyond, 'See you tomorrow ... today ... later.'

Sergeant Firth took Connie to the airport lounge while he went home to fetch some shoes for her from his thirteen-year-old daughter. 'Meena will keep an eye on you,' he said. 'She's cleaning the loos next door.'

When he'd gone, Connie took Hue out of his pouch. She set him gently on the floor to stretch his legs and broke a leaf off a pot plant for him to nibble. Then, putting him back in the pouch, she sat on a sofa and leaned back. It was so comfortable, and she was so exhausted, that the next thing she felt was a wake-up tap on the shoulder.

'Breakfast.' Meena was standing in front of her with a plate of bacon, eggs and toast on a tray. 'Eat up, love. Sergeant Firth says your flight's in an hour.'

He'd booked two tickets so that he could see Connie safely home. When she'd thanked him for his daughter's slightly too-big trainers, and said goodbye to Meena, they walked to the plane. He told her that they'd charged James Casey with the impressive-sounding crimes of unlawful restraint and attempted unethical human experimentation. 'And I phoned your mum to say we'll arrive in Dublin at nine thirty.'

It wasn't until Connie was in her seat that she realised, for the second time in just a few hours, she hadn't said, 'Actually, it's foster mum.'

— · —

An hour later they were walking through the Arrivals doors at Dublin airport. Mags stood behind the barrier, gripping the rail with both hands and looking like a thundercloud with a headache. She rushed round the barrier and pulled Connie into a hug.

'Mind Hue,' Connie gasped, hoping Sergeant Firth wouldn't hear. Luckily he'd hung back politely.

Mags stepped back, still grasping Connie's shoulders as if holding her together. And perhaps she was, because Connie suddenly felt that if Mags let go, she'd collapse in the middle like an under-baked cake. Blinking back tears, she caught sight of Thyo standing behind the barrier. His face was a tangle of relief, worry and guilt. Beside him stood Abri, then Naledi and Ned. And beside Ned stood Joe – Mr Dooley.

Mags cupped Connie's face in her hands. 'You stupid, crazy, idiotic – oh, thank goodness!' Tears ran down her cheeks. She gave Connie a little shake, whether out of joy or anger it was hard to tell, then ushered her to the barrier. The Miles family crowded round.

'Oh, Connie!' cried Naledi, kissing her. 'Your poor, poor ... Mags.' She shook her head. 'We didn't have her number.'

'I had to tell them about our phone calls,' said Thyo, giving Connie a fierce hug. 'I kept calling you after the last one, but your mobile was off.'

'I lost it,' she said in a small voice.

Abri put a protective arm round her brother. 'We were so worried. I made him tell Ma and Dad.'

'Naledi phoned the Leeds police,' said Ned, 'and they told her you were safe with a policeman at the airport.'

Connie had forgotten Sergeant Firth, who was standing behind her, smiling awkwardly. She introduced him.

'How can I thank you enough?' Mags gave him a hug, which should have been embarrassing but wasn't, because Naledi did too.

'We phoned the airport around midnight,' said Ned, 'to try and get Mags's number. But there was no answer. So we came here first thing this morning.'

'I was already here,' said Mags. 'With Joe.'

'Joe?' Connie couldn't help asking. 'You mean Mr Dooley?'

'I mean Joe,' said Mags. She clutched Connie's hand. 'I wanted to phone you so badly yesterday, to see how you'd got on filming. But I stopped myself, after ...' She sniffed. 'After what you said about being a proper mum.'

Connie dropped her eyes, guilt spilling inside her.

'I thought ...' Mags gave a smile that turned into a sob. 'I thought you might call *me*. I held off until nine o'clock. Then I tried, but your phone was off.'

Because I was tied to a chair. Connie shivered.

'I tried again at nine thirty,' said Mags.

When I was hiding inside a giant S.

'And at ten.'

When I was socking it through Leeds.

'I gave up, thinking you'd be in bed. Then—' Mags pressed a hand to her mouth. 'Sergeant Firth phoned in the middle of the night.'

Connie was astonished to see a hand appear on Mags's shoulder. A big, chunky hand with thick, leathery fingers: the sort of fingers that would be good at feeding hedgehogs without minding the prickles. 'Mags came in early this morning,' said Joe. 'She was so upset. Told me everything.' He handed her an enormous hanky.

'Which wasn't much,' said Mags, blowing her nose. 'What on earth happened, Con?'

Where do I begin? Images swirled and words whirled round Connie's head. *Trainers ... chameleons ... the machine ... the locket ... the ledge.*

She looked round at the faces, tight with exhaustion and bright with relief, and felt like a buffalo that had trampled a field of lovely, fragile flowers. What had she put them through? How could she have done this to Mags, to Thyo, to all of them?

'I'm so very sorry,' she whispered.

She waited for the blast, the 'So you should be!', the 'Told you so!', the 'How dare you!' But instead Mags squeezed her hand and said softly, 'Me too.'

Sergeant Firth cleared his throat. 'I'll, ah, let you folks catch up. Then I'll have a quick chat about the next steps in the investigation before I fly back.'

Naledi put her arms round Thyo and Abri. 'Connie and Mags have a lot to talk about. Let's go, guys.'

'No,' said Connie. 'You deserve to hear everything.'

So they went across to Pie in the Sky. Sue happened to be mopping the floor beside the café. She had a beady-eyed, hungry look, like a seagull circling for chips of gossip. Seeing Joe's hand on Mags's back, her mouth pursed into an even prunier prune than usual.

'Sue,' said Joe kindly but firmly, 'perhaps you'd take Sergeant Firth for a nice cup of coffee?'

Sue blinked at the policeman. Then she smiled and straightened her back, as if filling up with the importance of her task.

Ned pulled two tables together while Naledi brought over a tray of scones from Dave.

Everyone sat in wide-eyed silence while Connie told them everything, from smuggling Hue through airport security to James's arrest in Leeds.

When she'd finished, no-one moved – it seemed no-one *breathed* – until at last Thyo whispered, 'Wow.'

'Lord,' said Ned.

'Eish,' murmured Naledi, and Abri made a noise like 'Whoowf.'

Joe mumbled, 'Well, I'll be ...' before his mouth fell open and the end of the sentence sailed off in wonder.

Mags pressed a fist to her mouth and said absolutely nothing at all.

Thyo reached across to the tray. But instead of taking a scone, he pinched out a sultana.

'My diary entry,' he said, holding it up between his finger and thumb. 'For the day my best friend came home.'

41. Happy Birthdays

In English lessons last year, Mrs Farrell had told the class not to use clichés. 'Avoid them like the plague' was her little joke, which only Kate Mullins laughed at. But after Connie had shared her story, she really did feel like she'd 'got everything off her chest': as if a boulder of deceit and defiance had rolled off, letting her stand up straight again.

Almost. There was one more thing to confess. But not in front of Joe. Connie couldn't face that. So she waited until they were driving home. Sitting in the passenger seat, she stared carefully ahead. 'You know when Joe was rude to you?' she began.

'I do,' said Mags.

'Well.' Connie scraped her top teeth over her bottom lip. 'It was my fault.'

'I know,' said Mags.

'You do?' Now Connie couldn't help turning to stare at her.

And, wonder of wonders, Mags was smiling! 'When I came in all upset this morning, he was so kind. And while we were waiting for your plane, he apologised for being so unfriendly lately. He said he was hurt and annoyed because he'd sorta got the feeling I liked him, but then you told him I already had a man-friend.'

Connie felt heat flood her face, 'It was horrid of me. I was just so—'

'Angry. 'Course you were. I deserved it.' Mags reached over and patted her knee. 'And now you've come clean, it's my turn.'

Connie had to wait until they got home to find out what that meant.

'You go and sort Hue out,' said Mags as they walked through the front door. 'I'll be in the kitchen.'

Connie went upstairs. 'Home sweet home,' she said, opening the cage door. As she lifted Hue out of his pouch and on to a branch, Peter and the other chameleons crept across her mind. 'Please may they be OK,' she murmured. Surely they would be? Even if James had locked them back inside their cages, he wouldn't have had time to experiment on them before being arrested. 'And then they'll be rescued, Huey, and taken to some brilliant zoo where there are so many leaves and branches and crickets, and so much warmth and water and space, that it's not like a zoo at all, but a chameleon paradise.'

It would be ridiculous to say that Hue looked jealous. But as he turned and vanished into the foliage, she could swear his back glowed greener.

— · —

Mags was sitting at the kitchen table. She stood up as Connie came in. 'I'm so very sorry,' she said quietly, 'that I kept these from you.' Pressing her lips together, she walked out.

There were five cream envelopes on the table. They were all addressed to Connie in familiar handwriting.

Slowly she pulled out a chair and sat down. Slowly she took each envelope and lifted the already-opened flaps. Each contained a card with a chameleon on the front, below the words 'Happy Birthday'. One card showed a chameleon with a tail that dangled and coiled in the shape of a 6. On another card, a chameleon sat on a big number 7. A third card showed two chameleons with their bottoms facing each other and their tails entwining upwards in an 8-shape. On a fourth card, a chameleon hung upside down, its body forming the stalk of a 9 and the curled-up end of its tail the circle. The last card showed a chameleon wearing a rainbow party hat that bore the number 10.

Connie laid her palms on her lap. She sat very still, gazing at the pictures. Then she took the card for her sixth birthday, opened it and read the message inside. She replaced it on the table and took the next card. She read it and replaced that too. She did the same for all the cards. Then she did it all over again. When she'd read them three times, she slipped the cards back in their envelopes and piled them back on the table.

Dad's greetings were dull and spare, giving nothing away: the sort of things a distant, indifferent uncle might write.

Have a lovely birthday

Hope you have a great time

Enjoy your special day

But if he *was* indifferent, why had he written at all?

Connie sat for a long time looking at the pile, letting the colours of her feelings wash through her: angry reds, brown sweeps of sorrow, dark grey disappointment and purple-blue swirls of confusion. At last a quiet, calm green settled inside, as it dawned on her that perhaps there could be another reason for his meagre words. Perhaps they were the only ones possible for a man so sick with grief and guilt that he no longer trusted himself. Perhaps, by saying so little, he was trying to protect her: to show that he cared without writing anything that could risk inflaming the wounds of her past. Perhaps, between those skimpy lines, was all the love in the world for the daughter he'd failed.

And that's what she decided to believe. She could fill in the gaps between the facts of her dad with anything she chose. And what she chose was love.

She rose from the table and went into the sitting room.

Mags was on the phone. 'That's very kind of you,' she was saying, 'it sounds exciting. But I really can't take more time off work. And I have another appointment tomorrow afternoon. Anyway,' she looked at Connie and gave a sheepish little smile, 'this is Connie's adventure. She doesn't need me around. I'll wait to see her on telly so I can boast to all my friends.'

When she'd finished the call, she said, 'That was Naledi. We swapped numbers this morning before you flew in.'

It was Connie's turn to smile sheepishly.

'Apparently,' said Mags, 'the film director really *does* want you over there tomorrow to interview you about your fossil find.'

'Really?'

'And Ned wondered if you'd bring Hue. They invited me as well, but I thought I'd leave you to it, eh? You won't need me fussing about.'

Connie's smile broadened. 'Thank you,' she said, and, *Phew*, she thought. Mags's resolution to relax might fail if she saw Connie scaling a cliff.

They sat together on the sofa. 'What's your appointment tomorrow afternoon?' said Connie.

'Oh.' A little blush tickled Mags's cheeks. 'Joe's invited me over after work. He wants me to meet Mr Spickles.'

42. The Best Story

Connie was surprised to see Naledi standing on the doorstep with Thyo next morning. 'I thought Ned would collect me,' she said. 'Aren't you busy at the site?'

Naledi laughed. 'Not as busy as he is. And he's looking forward to seeing Hue.' She nodded at the travel box in Connie's hand.

Arriving at the mobile home, they found Ned sketching furiously at the table. Sure enough, he grinned at the sight of the box. 'Hue will help me get the skin texture right.'

Connie whooped. 'You've agreed to draw the dinosaur! I knew Hue would charm you into it.'

'Well, I wouldn't quite say *charm*.' Ned cleared his throat as she bent over to unclip the lid. 'You can, ah, keep him in the box. I can see him fine in there.'

She left him to it and followed Thyo and Naledi to the fossil site to meet the film director.

Brent Masterson was tall and hunched with a beaky nose, like an underfed vulture. His voice was raspy and his handshake dry. 'So you're the mountain goat who's going to climb our cliff.'

Mountain goat? Connie dropped her hand. That was how James had described her mum. Was it true, or just more of his make-believe? And what about the rest: had she really loved musicals and turquoise, hot chocolate and salt and vinegar crisps? Connie felt an ache like an inside bruise. There was so much she'd never know about her mum. Or her dad, except for those few precious memories which she would preserve for ever, like ... she gazed up at the cliff. *Like fossils.* Had he really wanted her to erase them? She'd never know that either.

But I do know he loved me, she reminded herself – as she would keep reminding herself every single day. It might not be the kind of knowledge she could prove with facts or figures, but every time she chose to believe it, the certainty would settle more deeply in her blood, her body and her brain.

Brent turned to Naledi. 'Run me through the dino-saur attack again. It's the climax. We need big drama.'

'Our theory is that the Megalosaurus killed the mother first, then smashed the eggs.'

'Hang on,' said Connie. 'How do you know it was a mother? It could have been a dad.'

Naledi raised her eyebrows. 'Well, obviously mothers are more likely to protect their young.'

'Are they?'

Brent gave a laugh like sandpaper on wood. 'Dad defending the babies for a change? I like it.'

'And how do you know,' Connie went on, 'that all the eggs were smashed by the Megalosaurus? What if one egg hatched before the attack? And while the father was defending the nest, what if the baby escaped?' She was talking more loudly and quickly. 'And what if it was found by another dinosaur who took it in and raised it as its own? And what if it went on to live a great life and to climb mountains and to love its foster parent like a real mum without ever forgetting the dad who had died trying to protect it?'

Three of the film crew had turned to gape.

'Because the truth is,' she gabbled unstoppably, 'we don't know what really happened. All we have is a fossil skull with a claw stuck in it and a bunch of broken eggs. The rest is just filling in the gaps with our own story. So why don't we make it the best story we can?' She blinked around at the silent, startled faces.

And suddenly she wanted to laugh. 'I'm going for a walk,' she said, turning round to hide her wobbling mouth. She marched along the beach, feeling hot and silly and full of bubbles that threatened to lift her into the air and send her floating over the sea.

Thyo found her on a rock, smiling into the distance. 'You look miles away,' he said, sitting beside her. She turned her smile on him.

'Which is funny,' he went on, 'because we're the Mileses, and we'll be away when the filming's done.'

Connie grabbed a piece of seaweed and was about to whack him when she saw his face. For once there was no grin, just a collision of his eyebrows. 'Ma's been asked to go to Namibia to look at some fossil or other.'

Connie knew nothing about Namibia except that it was beyond France. Her smile vanished.

'I told you it's not worth making friends.' Thyo snatched the seaweed and threw it into the sea.

— · —

Back at the mobile home, Connie knocked on the door of Abri's bedroom. 'No!' came her voice. 'You know you're banned, stinko.'

'It's me,' said Connie.

'Oh.' There was a scuffling sound. Abri's head appeared round the door under an orange sunhat. 'Sorry. Come in.'

'It's OK. I just wanted to thank you for calling the police in Leeds.'

'No worries.' Abri smiled. 'Hey, now you're here, can I get a photo of you with Hue? In fact – yes! In matching colours. That would make a great cover for my portfolio. You can borrow some clothes. I've got everything you need.'

And that gave Connie an idea.

— · —

'Super,' said Mags that evening. Which was lovely but not much help: first because everything Connie said or did had been 'super' since she'd come home, and second because Mags wasn't senior enough to organise it.

But Joe was. And that *was* helpful because he happened to be sitting next to Mags on the sofa. She'd invited him for dinner after their afternoon with Mr Spickles.

'I can ask the boss,' he said. 'I'll phone him now, if you like.'

Connie did like, which meant that Mags liked too, which meant that Joe trotted into the hall to make the call.

He came back beaming. 'All sorted. Mr Ryan said it'll be a breath of fresh air. His divorce has just come through and he could do with something to brighten his day. Abri can have all the space she needs.'

43. Plane Truths

When Connie and Mags arrived at the airport next morning, Abri waved from a table at the café. Then she ran across the Arrivals hall and hugged Connie. 'You're the best.'

'See you at lunch time,' said Mags and headed off to the lifts for work. Connie followed Abri to the table, where Thyo and Ned were waiting.

'Thanks for the loan,' said Ned. He took Hue's box in one hand, and his sketch pad in the other, and went to a seat beyond the café where he could open the lid and draw Hue, safely hidden from Dave's disapproving glances.

Connie helped all morning, sticking Blu Tack on the back of Abri's photos, until she came to one picture in the pile.

Her heart flipped.

There was the café in Terminal 2 where Mags had caught them, thanks to Sue. There was Connie, gripping the back of a chair like the handrail of a roller-coaster car. There was Mags with her ice-block face. And there was James, spreading his arms. The man prepared to risk her life for ... what? His fame and fortune if the memory-wiper worked? A genuine desire to help those in pain? Or both? Did he really think the machine was safe – that testing her was just a formality – or was he happy to sacrifice her for money, or for what he believed was the good of others? She stared at his eyes, dark behind their glasses ... with self-serving greed or scientific zeal? She'd never know.

What she *did* know, though, was how grateful she was to be home, safe with Mags and the memories that helped to make her the Connie she was.

At a quarter to one, airport staff began to gather. Dave laid out scones on a table and tea and coffee urns along the café counter.

'Are they free?' asked Andy from security who'd already eaten a scone.

'Just this once,' said Dave, in the grumpiest act of kindness Connie had ever seen. Seeing Ned come up with Hue's box, he scowled. 'Except for chameleons.'

'Well!' gasped a cleaner Connie only knew by sight, looking at a photo on the wall. 'I never gave permission to photograph my backside. I could charge you for usage rights.'

Connie hadn't thought of that. She glanced anxiously at the photo.

But Abri smiled. 'Go ahead,' she said breezily, 'if you can prove it's yours.' As Connie looked more closely, she saw there was nothing to identify the bent-over bottom in the grey trousers worn by all the cleaners.

And looking round the photos they'd put up in the hall, Connie saw how clever Abri had been. She'd either photographed her family, or strangers and staff at angles that made them unrecognisable, or people like Mags who'd given their permission, or Connie who wasn't going to object.

At one o'clock Mr Ryan arrived, along with Naledi and Brent Masterson. Naledi waved at Connie and Thyo, then rushed over to Ned in the corner to whisper something in his ear.

Mr Ryan clinked a cup with a teaspoon. 'Ladies and gentlemen, boys and girls and chameleons. It's my great pleasure to launch *Plane Truths*, the photo-story exhibition by Abri Miles. There will be a prize for the best story invented to explain any one of the photos. Grab your pens and off you go.' He turned to Sue, who'd brought him a scone and was smiling and chattering away. It seemed she had little trouble shifting her attention from Joe to someone of higher status.

Connie and Thyo explored the photos together. There was Connie wearing Abri's blue-and-green-striped dungarees and red polo neck, holding Hue with his blue-and-green-striped back and red legs. There was Joe talking to Sue but looking at Mags whose back was turned. There was Connie glaring after Thyo as he ran off to the toilet for disabled people. There was Connie hugging him across the café table after Not-Dad's first email. There was Hue's red foot above Ned's pale hand in the mobile home. There was Mags mopping the floor in Terminal 1 Departures, and there was Abri bending over a toilet with a loo brush in her hand, in a photo that Mags must have taken.

Thyo had just written the story behind it, as he imagined it – 'Jealous of her brother's good looks and intelligence, a girl flushes him down the toilet' – when Ned and Naledi came up, hand in hand.

'What?' said Thyo.

'A question,' said Ned.

'For you,' said Naledi.

'How would you feel—'

'About staying here?'

'What?' said Thyo again.

'I've been offered a job,' said Naledi. 'A permanent one, at the university, as Professor of Palaeontology.'

'It means we'd settle down here,' said Ned. 'I'd find some work. We'd buy a house.'

Thyo opened his mouth. But before he could speak, Naledi said, '*With* a garden.' Thyo closed his mouth.

'Abri would go to college,' she said, 'and we'd find a secondary school for you.' She turned to Connie and winked. 'Any recommendations?'

'Well,' said Connie, as sunshine exploded in her chest, 'there's a great school called St Peter's. I'll go and get the phone number from ...' She stopped and looked across the hall at Mags, who was laughing at a photo with Joe. 'From my ma.'

Acknowledgements

Writing a story feels a little like digging up a dinosaur. The bones lie buried, fossilised in layers of imagination and experience. It's the writer's job to unearth them, piece them together and flesh them out in her mind. And there's a team around her that cleans, examines and helps align the parts into a coherent whole. I am hugely grateful to the Little Island team, who have shaped and sharpened this book with such kindness and fun: Matthew Parkinson-Bennett, Siobhán Parkinson, Elizabeth Goldrick and Kate McNamara. Many thanks to Venetia Gosling for chiselling through the debris, to Emma Dunne for brushing up the remains, and to Rosa Devine for setting them in place. Ned Miles would be as thrilled as I am with ShannonBergin's beautiful cover that brings Connie, Hue, Thyo and Mags so vividly to life.

Thank you to all who have helped birth this book, from tutors, friends and fellow geology students at university to those who have cheered me on when the ground got muddy, especially Vera McEvoy, Martina Murphy, Sharon Ross and Doreen Philip.

To Nomfusi Joyce Baba, my dear South African mama and mentor who, with proper opportunities, could have been a palaeontologist or a president

To all the teachers, librarians, children and young people around Ireland who create on the page and inspire my days, especially the pupils and staff at Our Lady's Hospital School, Crumlin. It's an honour to work and wonder with you.

To Cynthia, Kenneth, Jenny, Hilary and family for your constant encouragement.

To my fabulous dad whose fossil-hunting adventures are highlights of my childhood; I'm still more excited by fool's gold than the real stuff. And to my brilliant mum who brought us up on kindness, curiosity, love and laughter.

To Jo and Iain. Your courage, generosity and strength of spirit are magnificent.

To Emily, Ruby and Rosa, the joys of my heart, the lights of my life and the knees of my bees.

And to Stevie my lodestone ... to go all geological again, what can I say but you rock?

ALSO BY DEBBIE THOMAS

MY SECRET DRAGON

A thrilling adventure story with a big heart, about family, friendship, being different – and baking!
Aidan Mooney has the mother of all problems. His mum is part-dragon.

He's spent his whole life struggling to keep her hidden from the world. But now, with the help of his super-smart new friend Charlotte, Aidan discovers a much darker secret hiding in the woods ...

'A smashing romp. The writing is excellent.'
– *Celine Kiernan, author of* Begone the Raggedy Witches

'Unforgettable characters and page-turning action.'
– *ER Murray, author of the* Book of Learning *trilogy*